ROBERTA GRIEVE

THE MIDNIGHT DANCERS

Complete and Unabridged

LINFORD
Leicester

First published in Great Britain in 2016

First Linford Edition
published 2017

A catalogue record for this book is available
from the British Library.

ISBN 978–1–4448–3257–0

Published by
F. A. Thorpe (Publishing)
Anstey, Leicestershire

Set by Words & Graphics Ltd.
Anstey, Leicestershire
Printed and bound in Great Britain by
T. J. International Ltd., Padstow, Cornwall

This book is printed on acid-free paper

1

Joanne came in from the kitchen and handed a mug of coffee to her sister.

'Anything in the paper, Liz?' she asked, putting her mug on the table and throwing herself down in the armchair next to her sister.

'Not much,' Liz replied.

Joanne leaned across and grabbed the property section but after a few moments she threw it down with a sigh.

'I'm never going to find a house,' she said. 'At least, nothing I can afford.'

'I don't know why you have to move anyway,' Liz said. 'You've been happy here.'

'It's not the same now Tom's gone.' Joanne choked back a sob.

'But they say you shouldn't make any big decisions too soon.'

'It's been two years, Liz. That's hardly too soon.' She sighed. 'I've tried to carry on for Lucy's sake. She doesn't want to move but she'll be going away to university in October and I'll be on my own. Besides, this house is far too big.'

'I remember when you and Tom bought it. You had such plans.' Liz gave a little laugh. 'Four kids wasn't it? And there's me, the career girl, ending up with a houseful.'

'You never know how things are going to turn out, do you?' Joanne said, with a sigh. 'Anyway, I've made up my mind. I'm moving.'

'Will you be looking for something nearer the college, then? I know you hate that long drive to work.'

'It's not so much the distance, it's the traffic. I'm always late these days, no matter how early I leave. Besides, I'm thinking of changing jobs too. I need to earn more money now.'

'Are things that bad then? I thought the insurance money paid off the mortgage.'

'Not quite, and the house needs a lot of work. Besides, it costs a bomb to heat and we don't use half the rooms.'

'I suppose it makes sense.' Liz finished her coffee and stood up. 'It's your decision, love. I hope you find something soon. Just don't move too far from me.' She gave Joanne a hug. 'Now, I must be off to pick the kids up from school.'

When her sister had gone, Joanne picked up the newspaper again. She had viewed so many houses lately but none of them had felt right. If she was going to leave her home after so many happy years, it had to be the right place.

I give up, she thought, and turned to the jobs page. Perhaps she'd have more luck here. Not that she held out any real hope — job-hunting these days was even harder than house-hunting. Still, she might as well have a look. She had to find a full time post soon, before her money ran out.

She leaned back in her chair and closed her eyes, letting the paper slide to the floor. If only Tom were here to help her with these decisions. But then, if he were, she would not be contemplating leaving her home of twenty years, or moving on from her job as library assistant at the college in the next town.

A slow tear leaked onto her cheek and she swiped it away impatiently. No good sitting here feeling sorry for herself. And no good getting angry with Tom for leaving her either. His heart attack at far too young an age had come completely out of the blue. He'd always been fit and active, and they'd had no idea of the congenital defect which had been lurking in the background.

The last two years had been hard, coping with a grieving teenage daughter, as well as her own grief, not to mention the worry over bills and repairs to the house. It was time to pull herself together and do something about it. Changing jobs would be a step in the right direction.

She sat up and retrieved the paper. Folding the pages, a headline caught her eye.

'Grayling Heir Found'
'New owner aims to restore Grayling Manor'

Joanne had always been intrigued by the

old manor house which stood at the top of the hill on the outskirts of town. It was near one of her favourite childhood picnic spots. There, through the dense trees, were tantalising glimpses of what she had always imagined as a fairy tale castle. It was sad that such a lovely old building had been left to decay for so long, she thought.

She sat back to read the article, pushing her niggling worries to the back of her mind as she became absorbed in the story of Clive Grayling, the Canadian heir to the Manor, and his ambitious plans for his ancestral home.

Opening to the public — *and* an art gallery. Some hopes, Joanne thought, remembering the state of the old house last time she'd passed that way. It would take an awful lot of time and money. Perhaps he'd won the lottery. For a few moments she indulged herself in day-dreams of winning the lottery herself but was brought abruptly out of her reverie by the slamming of the front door and her daughter calling out, 'Mum, I'm home.'

No need to tell me, dear — I heard you, Joanne thought with a smile. How she would miss Lucy when she went away.

Her daughter burst into the room, flinging her school bag onto the sofa and throwing herself down beside it. 'Thank goodness, that's over! Last day of school. I can get rid of this at last,' she said, pulling at her hated uniform blazer.

Joanne smiled. 'I can't believe it. It seems like only yesterday I was dropping you off at primary school.'

'Oh, Mum!' Lucy groaned, jumping up and taking her blazer off. She hung it over the back of a chair. 'What about you? Have you and Auntie Liz been looking at houses again?'

'Just one, but I didn't like it much.'

'Do we have to move? It seems … Oh, I don't know.' She sighed. 'I keep thinking about Dad and the happy times we've had here.'

'I do understand, Lucy. But this place is too big now, and expensive to run. Besides, wherever we are, we'll still have our memories.'

6

'I suppose so.' Lucy didn't sound convinced and Joanne felt a stirring of sympathy for her daughter. She *did* understand; she felt the same herself. But she had to be practical.

To change the subject, she stood up and said, 'I'll get the tea ready.'

Lucy followed her into the kitchen. 'I forgot to ask. How is Auntie Liz?'

'She seemed OK today — you know she has her ups and downs. But the sooner she gets this operation over with, the better.'

'She seems to have been waiting forever. It can't be easy for her with Uncle Mike away so much.'

'And coping with three kids. I don't know how she'll manage in the summer holidays. I'll help out if I can, but if I get a full time job, or if we're in the throes of moving ... ' Joanne's voice trailed off.

'You'll cope, Mum. You always do,' Lucy said, giving her a hug.

'Thank you for the vote of confidence.' Joanne managed a laugh.

Lucy gave her a little push. 'Go and sit down, Mum. I'll get the tea. Have another look in the paper — there might be something.'

Reluctantly, Joanne agreed, although she knew that yet again her daughter would be serving up microwaved pizza for their meal. She skimmed through the advertisements but nothing appealed — or if it did, would not pay more than what she was earning at the moment. It looked as if she might be forced to take a second part-time job, if she could only find one to fit in with her present hours.

She was about to give up when a small box at the bottom of the page caught her eye: archivist needed at Grayling Manor! Her heartbeat quickened. This could be it, she thought. But did she qualify? Still, the advertisement didn't say you needed a degree or any special qualifications. And surely her experience as a library assistant would help?

It was just the sort of job she'd always dreamed of, but could she honestly call herself an archivist? Still, it was worth a try. She loved the thought of handling fragile ancient documents and learning the history of the old house which had so often stirred her imagination. Perhaps her enthusiasm would overcome any short-comings in the qualification department.

There was only one way to find out. She grabbed her phone and dialled the number before she could change her mind. It rang for a long time and while she waited she couldn't help thinking that perhaps this was meant. She had just been reading about Clive Grayling and his plans to renovate the Manor but she could so easily have missed the ad tucked away at the bottom of the page.

Lost in thought, she'd hardly had time to think of what to say when a voice with a Canadian accent barked in her ear.

'Grayling. What is it?' She hesitated and before she could answer the man said again, 'Well, what is it?'

She swallowed. 'It's about the job — in the paper,' she stammered.

The man gave a short laugh. 'The job, you say? That was quick. It only went in the paper today.'

He must think I'm desperate, Joanne

thought, clearing her throat and putting on her best professional voice.

'Yes, Mr Grayling. It's lucky I saw it. I read about your plans for the Manor and I'm very interested.'

He was silent for a moment and she held her breath. Now he's going to ask about qualifications, she thought.

To her surprise he didn't.

'Interest and enthusiasm are what I'm looking for, plus a little bit of common sense, and last but not least, some experience of databases.'

'I think I can offer all of those,' Joanne said.

'Sounds great. How about coming up to the Manor for a proper chat. I can show you round and we can talk terms and conditions, whatever.'

Joanne said she would email her CV and ask the college for a reference and they arranged to meet the following day. She put the phone down, relieved that it had seemed so easy. After his initial abruptness, Clive Grayling had seemed OK, but she would see what he was really like when they met face to face.

She rushed into the kitchen to tell Lucy, her face aglow with excitement.

'I think I might have a job! Well, I've got an interview anyway.'

'Where is it? You sound really keen.'

Joanne told her about the article she'd read. 'And then I saw the ad,' she said. 'I thought it was worth a try.'

'Do you think you'll get it?' Lucy asked.

'I hope so. I've always been intrigued by the Manor. It's a shame it's been neglected for so long.'

They ate their pizzas at the kitchen table, and when they'd finished Joanne fetched the paper, folded back to the article.

'You remember it, don't you? We used to take you up there for picnics when you were small.'

Lucy quickly skimmed the page.

'It's a ruin though. Surely no one's going to actually live there,' she said, pointing to the grainy old photo of the

11

house, its towers wreathed in ivy. 'What happened to the owners?'

'I think they lost all their money and the family almost died out. The previous owner was living in one of the estate cottages.'

'You mean he just abandoned it?'

'It was used as a hospital or something during the last war and afterwards the owner never moved back in. Since then it seems to have been left empty. Mr Grayling said he's going to restore it.'

'He must have pots of money then.' Lucy laughed and crammed the last slice of pizza into her mouth. She picked up her plate and went over to the sink. 'Better keep in with him, Mum.'

'Don't be silly, Lucy,' Joanne said, smiling. 'Anyway, I'll find out more when I go for the interview.'

While they washed the dishes together they discussed what she would wear and speculated on the sort of questions Mr Grayling would ask.

'I hope I'm not being too ambitious,' Joanne said.

'Of course you aren't. You've always been interested in history and your experience of updating the library data-base should be enough. It seems to me you're just the person he's looking for,' Lucy reassured her. 'You must be in with a chance.'

Joanne still felt nervous though and she hardly slept that night.

The next morning she dressed carefully and paid more attention to her make-up than she usually did, trying to ignore her daughter's teasing.

'Sorry, Mum. I know you're nervous. Would you like me to come with you? I can wait in the car.'

'You're just nosy. You want to see what the new owner of the Manor is like,' Joanne said, teasing in her turn.

Lucy smiled. 'You could be right.'

★ ★ ★

The flint-faced mansion with its castle-like towers became visible through the trees and Joanne's heart missed a beat as she

13

started up the long winding drive, rutted and overgrown with weeds.

'I can't believe I might be working here before long,' she said.

'Fingers crossed, Mum,' Lucy said. But as the more of the house came into view, revealing missing roof tiles and encroaching ivy, she frowned. 'Are you sure about this? It's a ruin. It can't possibly be restored.'

'It might not be that bad inside,' Joanne said with an optimistic smile. She didn't want Lucy to sense her dismay.

The last time she had been out this way it had been with an estate agent to look at one of the old estate cottages which had recently come on the market. It hadn't grabbed her though. Despite her wish to downsize, it had been far too small. As she drove away she had caught a glimpse of the Manor through the trees and felt sad to see how neglected it was, although it hadn't looked too bad from a distance.

Now though, as she approached the main entrance she could see that it would take a great deal of work — and money

— to restore it to its original state. Was the new owner being too ambitious, as Lucy seemed to think?

She was almost tempted to turn the car around and go home but curiosity got the better of her. That, and the fact that she really needed to find a full-time, better-paid job. It wouldn't hurt to meet Clive Grayling and find out what was entailed. Besides, he might not even offer her the position and, if he did, she could always turn it down if she felt she couldn't work in such conditions.

2

'Well, here goes,' Joanne said, pulling up in front of the porch which was flanked by weather-worn stone animals. She laughed. 'I wonder if those are dogs or lions.'

'Could be either,' Lucy said. 'Well, go on, Mum. I'll wait in the car.'

Joanne shivered as she got out, her anticipation at seeing the interior of the old house waning a little. It would probably be freezing in there — a complete contrast to the cosy office she was used to.

She walked up to the front door and pulled at the bell set in the side of the porch, tapping her foot when there was no immediate response. She was about to try again when a man came round the corner of the house carrying a pair of shears. His dark hair curled over the collar of his open-necked shirt and his tanned face spoke of a life spent outdoors.

So, the new owner had already employed a gardener, she thought.

'Can you tell me where I can find Mr Grayling?' she called as he came towards her.

'You've found him,' he said, smiling and holding out his hand for her to shake. 'Sorry I didn't hear you ring. You must be Mrs Mason, come for the interview.' He ran his hand through his hair.

'Oh, I thought you were … ' Joanne began to stammer, feeling a flush rising up her neck. 'I thought you'd be older,' she amended.

'Old Mr Grayling, my great-uncle, passed on several years ago. You see before you the youngest and last of the Grayling dynasty.'

He led the way into the house and through a high-ceilinged Great Hall hung with crumbling tapestries and water-stained pictures. To one side a sweeping stone staircase led up to a landing lit by a stained-glass window that would not have been out of place in a cathedral.

'I hope you can manage to ignore all this,' Clive Grayling said, indicating their dilapidated surroundings. 'The old place is in a bit of a state — but not for long I hope.' He gestured to a small door set in an alcove behind the stairs. 'Come through. This is the oldest part of the house. Needs a lot of work but it's the only really inhabitable room so far.'

Joanne followed him into a room which was done out partly as office, partly a sitting room. The room was dark, with its oak beams and linenfold panelling, but a log fire crackled in the wide hearth giving a cosy and welcoming feel. Two armchairs were drawn up in front of it and she was grateful for the warmth after the chill of the hall.

'What a lovely room,' she said.

'It will be when it's finished. I've just done the bare minimum to make it habitable. This is actually part of the original manor house — Elizabethan, probably even a bit older. I'll know more when we start doing the research.'

'I'm looking forward to that. If you give

me the job, that is,' Joanne said.

'I think we can take it that you're hired.'

'What about references?' Joanne asked.

'I've read your CV. Besides, I like to make my own mind up about who I hire.' He grinned. 'Do sit down, Mrs Mason — or may I call you Joanne?'

'It's Jo,' she replied, used to the informality of her old job. She shrugged her coat off and sat in one of the armchairs near the fire.

'You'd better call me Clive then. I've been living in the wilds of Canada and we don't go in for formal there.'

'So I gathered,' Joanne said. 'This is not like any job interview I've had before.'

'It's not like any interview I've ever conducted either,' Clive said. 'I'm more used to dealing with roustabouts — you know, oilmen — not with attractive young women.'

Joanne's hackles rose but before she could think of a suitable retort he apologised. 'I'm sorry. My manners seem to have deserted me. I don't usually make remarks like that to women, married or not.'

'I'm a widow, Mr Grayling. Tom, my husband, died two years ago.'

'I'm so sorry.'

'I have a teenage daughter, and bills to pay. Which is why this job is important to me. So please, can we get on with the interview.' Best to be businesslike, Joanne thought. 'What exactly does the position entail?'

'I thought we could have an informal chat before getting down to business. But you're right, Joanne … Jo.' He cleared his throat. 'I'll fill you in on a bit of background. I hardly knew anything about the Sussex side of the family until very recently. I'd heard vague stories about a large estate in England but as I say, I grew up in Canada and my parents told me very little about how and why their grandparents emigrated. It was such a shock when I learned I'd inherited the Manor.'

Joanne was fascinated. She'd been intrigued by what she'd read in the local paper, which was partly why she'd applied for the job. It was a blend of curiosity and her love of architecture and history. She hadn't been able to resist the chance to be involved in bringing the old place back to life, even in a small way.

'So what are your plans?' she asked.

'Where do I start?' He ran his fingers through his hair and leaned forward. 'I want to restore the house, of course, but not just that. My great-uncle was a passionate collector of art. Most of it was sold for death duties, but I've found all sorts of stuff in the cellars and attics.'

'It's a wonder none of it was stolen,' Joanne said. 'Everyone knows the house is abandoned.'

'The solicitors employed a caretaker while they hunted for an heir. There was little money for repairs so all he could do was make sure the house was secure and keep the vandals out.'

'Seems strange to leave it like this, with all those tapestries and paintings,' Joanne said.

'As I say, the valuable stuff was sold.

21

The rest looks like worthless junk, or at least, it would to most people. It's all been damaged by damp and neglect, but it can be restored. My great-uncle was also patron to a few modern artists, not well-known in his day but they are becoming collectable now, and some of their work is in storage.'

'You want to turn Grayling Manor into an art gallery?' Joanne was confused. 'So why do you need me? I'm a librarian, not an art expert.'

'You said you were a cataloguer and know your way around computers. I want the pictures and furnishings catalogued and put on a database. And not just that — books, papers, letters, old account books, the lot.'

'I can do that,' she said, confidently. 'It sounds very interesting.'

'You mentioned an art gallery, and of course I will eventually have stuff on display for visitors,' Clive said. 'But my vision goes further than that. Some of the pictures might be worth a bit once restored, so I'll sell them and use the money to turn this house into a study centre for local history as well as the arts.' He stood up and began to pace the room, his enthusiasm reflected in his shining eyes and his expressive hand gestures. 'In time, I might even run courses — arts and crafts, restoration techniques. There are endless opportunities.'

Jo couldn't help being infected with his enthusiasm.

'It sounds exciting,' she said. Being involved in something like this was just what she needed after the difficulties of the past couple of years.

'I'll show you round,' he said, leading the way back into the Great Hall. 'Here's where the paintings and sculptures will be on display.' Scarcely giving her time to take it in, he rushed across to the stone staircase and beckoned her to follow. 'More of them up here in the long gallery,' he said.

At the top of the stairway a wide gallery led off to the left and right.

'This is the newer part of the house,' Clive said, gesturing to the array of floor- length windows along the one side. 'Not exactly new now, of course — it was added at the end of the 18th century, the whole frontage. As I said, originally Grayling Manor was just a modest Elizabethan house. When they built this bit they left the back part as kitchens and pantries, servant's quarters and such.'

'It's very impressive,' Jo said, appreciating the stonework and vaulted ceiling.

'I think the Graylings of the day wanted to impress with their wealth and status. Didn't last long though, did it?' he said, laughing. 'They lost most of their money and it's been downhill all the way since then.'

'It's a beautiful building though.'

'Well, it will be once the work's done,' Clive said. 'At the moment you can't really see much for dust and cobwebs, not to mention those patches of damp.'

'Seems like a lot of work. It could take years.'

'Not years — months. I aim to be open by this time next year.'

Joanne didn't reply. She admired his

enthusiasm but had her doubts about how feasible his plans were. Still, it wasn't her worry. At least it seemed she now had a job, but for how long, she wondered. Would he still need her once the house was open to the public? That's if it ever happened. Looking around as she followed Clive striding down the corridor, she tried hard to see past the dilapidated state of the place and picture it as he obviously did. As they progressed, he threw open the doors which punctuated the long gallery to reveal an impressive array of rooms, each with wide stone fireplaces and tall leaded windows.

She went across and looked out at the view of the South Downs in the distance, a scene she had always loved.

'It's beautiful,' she said, turning back into the room and shivering, wishing she'd kept her jacket on. She hesitated and then said, 'Surely it's going to take a great deal of money to do all this.'

Clive laughed. 'More than the sale of a few pictures will fetch, you mean.'

Joanne nodded, biting her lip, hoping

he wouldn't think she had been too outspoken.

'I did mention I was an oilman, didn't I? Well, I've made a bit of money over the years. I'm no Bill Gates, by any means, but I think I can do it.'

Just wait till I tell Lucy, Joanne thought, as he marched off down the corridor, beckoning her to follow.

He paused at the end of the passage, gesturing to a spiral staircase.

'We won't go up there today. I'm not sure it's safe. But the attics are crammed with stuff. It's going to take ages to sort it all out.'

'What sort of stuff?'

'Ledgers, letters, estate records, photographs. There's more in the cellars too, although I haven't really explored down there yet.'

'And that's what you want me to catalogue?' Joanne asked, craning her head to look up the dark, twisting stairs.

'Everything. Don't worry; you won't have to go up there. I've got workmen coming to bring everything down before they can start work on the plastering and damp-proofing.'

Joanne shivered but she managed a smile. 'It's like something out of one of those old black and white horror films.'

Clive laughed. 'I have heard a rumour that the place is haunted but I don't believe in such nonsense,' he said.

'Neither do I,' she said firmly.

'Good. Now, let me show you the rest of the house.'

The rest of the whirlwind tour left her breathless but fizzing with excitement. Back in the Great Hall, Clive said, 'Now for the bit that will really interest you — the library.'

He pushed open the heavy oak door and she gasped with delight. A carved stone fireplace dominated the centre of one wall and opposite that, tall windows looked out on to the grounds. The other walls were lined floor to ceiling with shelves crammed with books.

Joanne went over and pulled one of the books off the shelf, wrinkling her nose at the musty smell of damp. The corner of the cover was flecked with mould and she frowned, her love of books making her sad at this evidence of neglect. How could people leave stuff like this, she wondered.

'It's a shame, but most of these will have to be thrown out. Although we might be able to restore some,' said Clive. He gestured to the large table under the window. 'Here's where you'll be working — that's if you agree to come,' he said.

'You mean I've really got the job?' Joanne could hardly believe it. Surely there were more experienced archivists who would give their right arm for a chance like this? Perhaps she was the only one who'd applied.

'Yes, if you really want it after what you've seen. I mean, not everyone would fancy working in this cold, draughty old place. And it'll be a bit lonely, after working at the college with lots of people around.'

'I shan't mind that at all,' Joanne said.

'Well, it won't be cold for long. Installing a heating system is one of my top priorities; that and the roof.'

Joanne was pleased to hear it. The chill had been seeping into her bones as they toured the house.

Clive must have noticed her relief, and he grinned.

'I know it's supposed to be summer but I'm keeping fires lit all through the house to try and get rid of the damp. There will be a fire in here when you start work. You will be taking the job, I hope?'

'Of course. I can't wait.'

'When can you start?'

'The summer break is coming up now, so if I send in my notice straight away, I hope they'll accept and let me leave at once,' she said.

'Good. Let's go back in the warm and talk business,' he said, leading the way back to his cosy study.

'Why did they keep all that stuff, I wonder,' Jo said.

'These old families never throw anything out. The cellars are packed with bits of old furniture and then there's all the stuff in the attics. The house was used as a convalescent home for the military during the last war and afterwards it was left empty. My great-uncle went to live in one of the estate cottages.'

'I read about that in the local paper,' Joanne said. 'Why didn't he move back in when the war was over?'

'There was no money to keep this place up but he couldn't let it go.'

Jo was intrigued and was looking forward to finding out more about the family history when she got stuck into the archives. It promised to be a much more interesting job than the one she'd done before.

★   ★   ★

By the time she left, Joanne's head was reeling. Excited as she was at the prospect of being involved in Clive Grayling's vision for the future of the Manor, she did wonder if she might have bitten off more than she could chew. But she was smiling as she got in the car.

Lucy closed her tablet. 'You've got it,

then? I can tell,' she said.

Jo nodded. 'He wants me to start straight away. I'll have to let the college know I won't be back next term.'

'Did you ask about the pay?'

'Of course — and it's very generous. It'll make things easier for us.'

'Does that mean we won't have to move house?'

'I'm afraid not,' Joanne sighed and started the car. 'You know Dad's insurance didn't cover the mortgage. It's been a real struggle lately. I have no choice, Lucy.'

Lucy sighed. 'I suppose so.'

They were silent as Joanne negotiated the choked roundabout leading to the supermarket on the outskirts of town. If only she could find a house this side of the bypass, perhaps in one of the villages close to the Manor. One of her reasons for moving had been the stressful drive to work each day. But houses in this part of the county were usually quite out of her range.

'I'm pleased you got the job anyway,

Mum,' Lucy said, breaking the silence.

As she pulled off the roundabout onto the main road, Joanne was pleased her daughter sounded so positive, and interested for a change. She had been very moody lately, perversely disagreeing with everything Jo said. She understood of course — Lucy was missing her father, but like many teenagers found it hard to talk about her feelings, especially to her mother.

'I must admit I'm excited about it. It'll be quite a challenge. Let's hope I'm up to it.'

'You will be.'

Jo smiled and said, 'I can't wait to start.'

'What's the house like inside?' Lucy asked. 'Creepy, I bet. All cobwebs and mould. I wonder if it's haunted.' She gave a theatrical shiver and giggled.

'Don't be silly, Lucy. There's nothing creepy about it, although Mr Grayling did say the locals think there's a ghost. But he doesn't mind — it kept them away while the place was empty!'

'It will make a good story when he

opens to the public.'

'Mr Grayling has great plans. He wants to open an art gallery.'

Lucy became seriously interested. She was going to university to do an arts degree so the idea of her mother working in a gallery intrigued her. She turned to her mother with a grin.

'What's he like?'

'Nothing like I imagined,' Joanne said. 'He made his money from oil in Canada, but I think he's the sort of man who would have been out there in the field, working alongside the men — not stuck in an office totting up his profits and investments.'

'Doesn't sound like an arty type, then,' Lucy said.

'That's what I thought, but his enthusiasm seems genuine. And he's very interested in researching the history of his family and the Manor.'

'Right up your street then, Mum.'

Joanne nodded. 'Yes. I think I'm going to like it.'

'And Mr Grayling — do you think you'll

like him too?' Lucy's voice was flat, her earlier teasing manner replaced by a frown.

'He seems very nice.' Joanne tried to keep her tone neutral, knowing that her daughter resented the slightest hint at her mother's interest in a man. No one would ever replace her father and at this stage in her life Joanne agreed with her. Try convincing Lucy of that, she thought with an inward sigh. She changed the subject, asking about her plans for the weekend.

'Nothing much. I might meet up with Ben and the others,' Lucy replied.

'I thought you'd come and look at houses with me. I've got three viewings lined up.'

'Why would I want to do that? You know how I feel about moving.'

'Yes, you've told me enough times. But, Lucy, I really don't have a choice.' Joanne pulled up at the traffic lights and turned to her daughter, laying a hand on her arm. 'Look, love, I don't want to leave our home either, but it's just not practical to stay there now.'

Lucy hunched down in the seat and turned her face away.

Joanne could see she was trying not to cry and she pretended not to notice, putting the car in gear and pulling away as the lights changed.

A few minutes later they were held up at the railway crossing and she groaned. They'd never get home at this rate. She hoped one of the places she was due to look at would be suitable. At least they were in a more convenient location, especially now that she had landed the job at Grayling Manor — not nearly so far to drive.

They finally reached home and Lucy got out of the car without speaking. She grabbed her backpack, rushing upstairs the minute they were indoors.

Joanne decided to leave her alone and started to get a meal ready. When the food was on the table, she called Lucy down, and was relieved to see her smiling.

'Sorry, Mum. I know I'm being unreasonable. But I get upset just thinking about it.'

'Believe it or not, so do I,' Joanne said.

'I will come with you tomorrow, if you still want me to.'

'Oh, yes please. You've got to like the place too, you know. It'll be your home as well.'

'I suppose you're right. Although I won't be there all the time. I'll be off to uni in a few weeks, and after that — who knows?'

Relieved, Joanne cleared the table and got out the brochures. But as they leafed through them, discussing the various features of the houses on offer, she had a feeling that none of them would match up to her daughter's demands.

3

The long line of vehicles crept slowly towards the roundabout and Joanne sighed as she applied the brakes once more. The headache that had been building all day took hold and she felt sick. Even with sunglasses and the visor down, the lowering sun almost blinded her. And on top of that, the old car's air-conditioning had finally given up just when summer had finally arrived. It looked as if this was going to be the hottest day of the year so far. It was hard to adjust to the change after so many days of rain and chill winds.

'Mum, are you OK?' Lucy pulled her earbuds out, releasing a blast of music.

Jo winced.

'Sorry,' Lucy said, turning the sound down.

'I've got to get out of this traffic.'

'But it's not far now. Once we get on the main road ... '

'Lucy, my head's killing me. I can't drive like this.'

The car behind hooted impatiently and they inched forward again.

Lucy seemed to realise her mother wasn't feeling at all well.

'Let me drive. You can turn off into that lane,' she suggested.

Ignoring the blasts from the following cars, Joanne manoeuvred across and entered the lane. It was cool and shady under the trees and she stopped the car, relieved to be out of the glaring sunlight. She dropped her head onto the steering wheel and sighed.

'Mum?'

'I'll be all right in a minute.'

Lucy opened the door and got out.

'There's a seat over there. Come and sit in the shade.'

Joanne followed her to a wooden bench next to an old flint wall bordering a tiny church. She took a few deep breaths and looked around her, guessing that this had originally been part of the main road, cut off when it was straightened years ago. Just visible through the trees were several modern houses where the lane curved round to re-join the main road a bit further on.

'What a day,' she said.

'What a waste of day you mean,' Lucy said.

'I suppose so. Well, not really. We had to go and look. Shame none of them was the right house for us.'

'We've been looking for weeks. How many viewings have we done? I've lost count.'

'So have I. But there's always something not quite right.'

'What's wrong with our old house?' Lucy's mouth turned down. 'I still don't see why we have to move at all.'

It was an old argument and Joanne was losing patience.

'I've told you enough times. I can't afford to stay there.'

'It won't be the same, coming back in the holidays to a strange place.'

'It'll still be your home. You'll have your own room with all your things.'

'It's not the same,' Lucy repeated, a catch in her voice.

Joanne knew how she felt; until recently, she'd agreed. But since starting work at Grayling Manor she had finally started to feel that she was ready to move on. And moving house was part of that. But how could she make Lucy understand?

It wasn't just an emotional decision. There were practical reasons too, and not just financial. It made sense to move a little nearer to the Manor. She certainly couldn't continue to face the rush hour traffic every day.

It was no use going over the same old ground again though. Lucy would just have to accept things. After all, when she'd got her degree, she'd be making her own way in the world, leaving Jo to try and make a life for herself on her own.

'I'm sorry, love,' she said. 'The house is under offer. We've got to move on.'

'Move on? How can you say that? It's too soon ... '

'Lucy, please.' Jo covered her face with

her hands. 'Let's talk about something else.'

Lucy stood up and stomped off down the lane. Jo let her go. She'd be back in a minute, Jo thought, used to these 'mini-strops', as she called them. She knew Lucy missed her father and the thought of also losing the home she'd grown up in seemed just another tragedy to her. But she was an intelligent girl and Jo was confident that once she got involved with university life and started to make new friends, she'd become reconciled to the new house — wherever that might be. She sighed again. The house-hunting had not gone well so far and it was becoming urgent that she find a place.

The traffic would hopefully be easing soon, so she looked around for Lucy. She must have gone into the churchyard.

Jo called out, tapping her foot and glancing at her watch. When there was no reply, she called again, becoming anxious when she was greeted by silence. A collared dove suddenly cooed from a nearby tree and she jumped.

'Lucy, where are you?' She took a few hesitant steps. 'Lucy, we need to go,' she shouted.

She pushed open the gate and walked along the overgrown path into a church-yard — a very overgrown and neglected one. She rounded a bend in the path and found herself in front of the church porch. She tried the door but it was locked. So where was Lucy?

She was about to call again when her daughter appeared round the side of the building.

'Mum, come and see. This is really interesting,' she said, seemingly unaware of Jo's anxiety.

'Never mind that. Where were you? I was getting worried.'

'Oh, Mum!' Lucy's voice was affection-ate, despite the laugh that accompanied it. She seemed to have forgotten her ear-lier discontent and pulled at her mother's arm. 'Look — isn't it lovely? This church is really old, you know. It might even be older than the Cathedral.' She pointed to a row of terracotta tiles set low in the wall. 'I reckon there was a Roman building here first. They must have used these when they built the church.'

Jo smiled; Lucy had inherited her love of history. She looked back towards the main road, realising that the roar of traffic was somewhat muted by the screen of trees.

'Do you know, I've driven along that road loads of times and never realised this church was here,' she said.

'It looks as if it's not used any more,' Lucy said. 'The notices in the porch are way out of date.'

'Such a shame. I wonder what will happen to it. It's too far out of town to turn it into a restaurant like the one in the Square.'

Lucy wasn't listening. She had wandered further into the churchyard, peering at the gravestones and reading out the epitaphs. Joanne followed, although it wasn't really something that interested her.

It was good that her daughter had cheered up though, she thought, noting the sulky expression had been replaced by smiles. A stinging nettle brushed against her calf and she bent to rub it, straightening abruptly as Lucy cried out, 'Oh, that is so sad.'

Jo hurried over and looked down at the three tiny graves in a row, each with a simple cross.

Lucy was kneeling down trying to read the inscriptions. She pulled a strand of ivy away, revealing worn letters carved in the stone. 'Edward B-L-A-something, aged eight years.' Her voice dropped as she tried to make out the other names. 'Oh, Mum, it's so sad.'

Jo pointed to the date. '1890. Children died young in those days,' she said. 'Perhaps there was an epidemic.'

'I know. It's still sad though.' Lucy moved along to a larger grave at the end of the row. 'Margaret Chapman, aged 21 years, 1890. The same date,' she read. 'I wonder what happened to them all.'

'We'll never know, will we? Come on, Lucy, we must be getting home.'

Lucy turned away and followed her

mother back to the car, but she kept looking back.

As they were about to get in, Jo noticed that the house next to the church had a 'For Sale' notice board propped up next to the gate. After spending so much time looking at houses, she was totally fed up with house-hunting. But her curiosity was aroused by the coincidence. It almost felt like it was meant to be, them stopping here. It couldn't hurt to take a look …

The house itself was set back from the road and almost hidden by the straggling hedge which is why she hadn't noticed it before. The name on the gate was 'The New Rectory' — rather an outdated name now, bearing in mind she was looking at a solid, 1920s era house, Joanne thought.

'Oh, no, Mum. Not another house,' Lucy groaned.

'Just a quick peek,' Jo said. 'It looks as if it's empty.' She strode purposefully up the path and peered through the front bay window into a large, well-proportioned living room. 'Needs decorating but it's in good nick,' she said.

'I thought we were downsizing. It's huge,' Lucy said.

'Not huge, Lucy. Maybe a bit bigger than I planned, but it's still smaller than ours. And stuck out here, needing a bit of TLC, the price could be right.' It was nothing like the specification she had given the estate agents but for some reason Jo felt a surge of excitement. She rummaged in her bag and found a pen and an old envelope, noted down the name and website of the estate agent. It wasn't one of those she'd been dealing with but she'd check the site when she got home.

Lucy was sulking again. Jo knew she'd been hoping that if they really had to move it would be to a house in town where she could meet up with her friends without having to ask her mother for lifts everywhere. But she wouldn't be living at home much longer. Jo had to think of herself for a change and this would be ideal for her, provided it didn't need too much doing to it. It was only a couple of miles from the Manor and, with no traffic lights, railway crossings or roundabouts in between, she'd be only minutes from work. She could even start cycling again.

Curbing her enthusiasm, she patted her daughter's arm.

'Don't worry, love. It's just a thought. I don't expect anything will come of it.'

'I hope not,' Lucy muttered, as they went back to the car.

They were about to get in when another vehicle pulled up and a man got out.

He smiled and came across to them. 'Come to look at the church?' he asked.

'Actually, I was just looking at the house,' Joanne admitted.

'Oh good. Someone's interested then.'

'I'm not sure. It looks a bit neglected.'

'Unfortunately, yes.' The man held out his hand. 'I'm Timothy Blake — Father Tim — rector of this parish. I used to live there.' He gestured towards the house.

'We thought the church wasn't used any more,' Jo said.

'We have a service once a month — a few stalwarts turn up,' he said. 'I'm joint rector with St George's in town, so I live there now.'

'The church is very old isn't it?' Lucy said.

'Parts go back to the 13th century or even earlier. If you're interested in old churches, I'd be happy to show you around.'

'That's kind, thank you. We haven't got time just now though, I'm afraid,' Jo said.

'Well, if you decide to buy the house, perhaps you'll come to one of our services.'

Jo smiled and said, 'Maybe.'

They said goodbye and got into the car.

'Some hopes,' Lucy said as she did her seatbelt up. She turned to her mother. 'You're not serious about that house are you?'

'Probably not. I was just curious, that's all.'

'Who wants to live next door to a graveyard anyway?'

Joanne laughed. 'You've got a point.'

But as she left the leafy lane and re-joined the main road, she could not get the house out of her head. In spite of it being rather larger than she'd planned to buy, its main advantage was that it was to the north of the busy A27 and its traffic problems. Perhaps the New Rectory would be the answer to her prayers.

4

There was a lot to get rid of and Jo had put off sorting out the house. It was hard to get rid of the accumulated memories of twenty years. She leaned back in her chair, rubbing her eyes. She'd switched on the computer to check her emails and, as usual, had spent far too long trawling the net.

There had been a couple of messages from estate agents but just a quick look had told her that the properties on offer were totally unsuitable — too expensive, too far away, too small. She had envisaged a small, two-bedroom house on one of the new developments that were springing up on the outskirts of town. But after spending most of her married life in a three-storey Edwardian villa facing the sea, all the places that she'd looked at seemed far too cramped. Now though, the house was sold and things were progressing rapidly. She really would have to find something soon, or move into a temporary rental.

So far she had resisted looking up the agent who was selling the New Rectory, telling herself that making a note of the website had just been a foolish impulse. But she couldn't get it out of her head. She had always thought of herself as sensible and down to earth, not usually given to flights of fancy. But something was drawing her to that house, even as she told herself she was in danger of letting her heart rule her head.

Giving in to impulse, she scooted her chair closer to the desk and typed in the name of the estate agent. It wouldn't hurt to take a look. Once she'd seen that the price was out of her league — as she was sure it would be — she could put it out of her mind and get on with some serious house-hunting.

The website popped up showing thumbnail pictures of desirable properties and Jo scrolled down.

'There it is,' she said aloud.

It looked much better in the photograph, until she enlarged it and saw the peeling paintwork around the windows. Far too much work needed. But then she saw the price, and it was a lot lower than she'd anticipated.

Without stopping to think, she picked up the phone and called the agent.

A man answered just as Lucy came into the room, leaning over Jo's shoulder to look at the photo on the screen.

'Mum, what are you doing?' she exclaimed.

'Shh!' Joanne waved her daughter to silence and spoke into the phone. 'Yes, I'm calling about the New Rectory, the house in Church Lane, just off the Winterbourne road.'

Lucy tapped her foot impatiently as she listened to her mother's end of the conversation and Jo frowned at her, shaking her head. She nodded into the phone.

'Yes, I'd like to arrange a viewing. Great! This afternoon, then? I'll meet you there at three.'

She put the phone down and turned to Lucy with a sheepish grin.

'We're only going to look, love. It doesn't mean I'll buy the place.'

'You're mad, Mum. We can't live there. Think of all the work it needs.'

'But at that price, I can afford it. And let's face it, Lucy, we've been looking for months and nothing anywhere near suitable has come up.'

'Well, you know how I feel about moving anyway.' The mutinous look was back on Lucy's face.

Jo sighed. She seemed to be sighing a lot these days. 'Yes. You keep telling me.' She switched off the computer and stood up. 'Please, Lucy. You'll come with me, won't you?'

'I suppose so. Perhaps I can persuade you what a mad idea this is.'

*　*　*

It was still hot but the traffic was much lighter so the drive to the New Rectory was far pleasanter than it had been the

53

previous week. Lucy's mood brightened somewhat as they got out of the car.

'I can see why you like it, Mum. It's a bit like Gran's old house, isn't it?'

'I hadn't thought of that, but yes, you're right. That little porch and the bay windows.'

'It's weird though, isn't it? I mean, it's not the sort of house you'd expect to see here; kind of out of place really.'

Jo pushed open the garden gate. 'The agent's here already, look.'

He came to meet them, clipboard at the ready, a conservatively dressed young man in suit and tie. He looked rather uncomfortable in the heat, but he greeted them cordially and led them up the path to the front door. Turning the key in the lock he said, 'As you can see, it is in need of a little refurbishment but nothing major. Just cosmetic really.'

A *little,* Jo thought, noting the peeling wallpaper and the cracked tiles on the hall floor. But the agent seemed keen to play down the less desirable aspects of the house, extolling the high ceilings, the curved banister, and the bay windows which let in lots of light, despite the encroaching undergrowth in the overgrown garden.

At least it's not as bad as the Manor, Jo thought, remembering the overpowering smell of damp and the swathes of cobwebs hanging from the vaulted ceilings. And she had to admit that this house did have some very attractive features. As they progressed, she became even more enthusiastic. The agent was right about the positive aspects and she found herself easily overlooking the work that needed doing.

She could see that Lucy wasn't keen though, despite her earlier comments. But then, she'd been against the idea of moving from the start. She'd found fault with every house they'd looked at. Too bad, Jo thought, as she made up her mind. This was it. Not exactly the house of her dreams but for some unknown reason she already felt at home here.

They reached the end of the tour and went back into the hall. As the agent opened the front door, Jo noticed the tiles.

'These are lovely,' she said. She looked up at the agent. 'I don't understand. These are clearly very old, much older than the house.'

The agent cleared his throat. 'They belonged to the earlier house. This one was built on the foundations.'

'How interesting. I don't suppose you know anything more about the earlier house? A little of the history of the place, perhaps?'

'Apparently, the original Rectory was one of those rambling old houses, lots of rooms. But I read somewhere that it burnt down. The plot was derelict for years. Then, in the 1920s, this was built on the site to house the rector again.'

He glanced down at his clipboard. 'Well, Mrs Mason, can I say you're definitely interested?'

His expression was a little anxious and Joanne thought he'd probably shown a lot of people round in the past months. It had obviously been on the market for ages.

'I am, but can I have a few days to think about it?'

'Take as long as you like.'

His relief was obvious and Joanne smiled. She had made up her mind but she didn't want to seem too eager. With a bit of luck, she might manage to negotiate a lower price.

Lucy gave an exclamation of disgust and walked away, shoulders hunched. Joanne shrugged and smiled at the agent.

'Teenagers!' she said.

He grinned and followed her back into the lane, pausing beside his car.

'You've got my card? And you'll be in touch?'

'Definitely.'

They shook hands and he drove away, leaving Joanne looking around for Lucy. Where had the girl got to now? Through the trees, she glimpsed her daughter examining one of the gravestones, as she had on their first visit. She seemed completely absorbed in the inscription.

'Come on Lucy,' she called. 'We'll get

caught in the rush hour again if we don't get a move on.'

The girl came towards her with dragging steps.

'You're really going to buy it, aren't you?'

'Probably,' Jo said.

'I don't want to live next to a graveyard. It's creepy.'

If it was so creepy, why was Lucy so fascinated by the gravestones? Joanne thought. She didn't comment though, and Lucy sulked all the way home.

* * *

Later that evening Jo phoned her sister.

'Liz, I've put in an offer on a house,' she said.

'Thank goodness you've found somewhere,' Liz said. 'Where is it?'

When Joanne told her, Liz laughed. 'Have you gone mad?'

'Possibly. Lucy thinks I have, anyway.' Joanne laughed too. 'But it's fantastic. Or at least it will be when I've finished with it. It's nearer to you, and it's got a lovely big garden. The kids will love it when I'm looking after them for your hospital stay.'

'But weren't you coming to stay here?'

'I've been thinking about it. If they stay with me it'll be easier to drop them off at school and then go on to work.'

'I suppose you're right. But will you be settled in by then?'

'Well, it's a while before you go in. I'll definitely have the kitchen and bathroom done by then. Don't worry, Liz. It'll be OK.'

'All right.' Liz paused. 'So, when do I get to see this fabulous house of yours?'

'I'm going to have another look next weekend, see what needs doing, start making lists. Why don't you and the kids come over on Saturday?'

* * *

When they reached the New Rectory, Liz looked up at the house, her face a mask of horror.

'Oh, Jo, what have you done? I thought you were downsizing,' she said.

'I told you, Mum,' Lucy said. 'You're mad. Auntie Liz thinks so too, don't you?'

Liz bit her lip. 'Well, going by first impressions, yes.' She got out of the car and opened the back door for the children. 'Lucy, can you keep an eye on the kids for me while your mum shows me round?'

'OK. Come on, you lot. Let's go and explore.'

Lucy and the three children disappeared round the side of the house and Liz turned to her sister.

'Let's see inside, shall we?' she said.

After making a firm offer and its being accepted, the estate agent had given Jo a key. Now, she took it out of her bag, marching up the overgrown garden path and throwing the door open.

'There. It's not as bad as it looks from outside,' she declared.

Liz raised her eyebrows. 'It's not exactly what you had in mind though, is it?' She ran her hand over the carved banister. 'Still, I can see it's got potential.'

'I can just picture it.' Jo's face shone with enthusiasm. 'I've got such plans. It'll be lovely once it's done up.' She rushed from room to room, pointing out the features she wanted to restore and the bits she would rip out and modernise.

'The kitchen and bathroom are priorities obviously. I'll get tradesmen in to do them. But the decorating I'll tackle myself. Lucy will be off soon and I'll be able to get on with it at weekends.'

Liz put her hand on her sister's arm.

'Are you sure about this? Jo. It's a lot to take on, especially with your new job as well.'

'I need to keep busy, Liz. Having a project like this will help me move on.'

'I suppose so. But what about when I go into hospital? You'll have my three to cope with as well.'

'I'll manage. Besides, they'll be back at school by then, won't they? You worry too much.'

Liz looked doubtful but she didn't comment, instead pointing to a door next to the kitchen. 'What's through there?' she asked.

'It used to be a sort of pantry or scullery I think.' Joanne opened the door to reveal a small room with a window looking out on to the side of the house. Any fixtures or fittings it had once held had been ripped out, leaving a bare shell.

'This is going to be my study,' she said.

Liz shivered. 'Better get some heating in here. It's freezing. If it's like this in summer, what will it be like later on?'

'It'll be fine once we've cut some of the shrubbery back. It's only dark and gloomy because it gets no sun at the moment.'

Liz went over to the window and peered through the grime.

'What's over there?' she asked.

'That's the churchyard. You can just see the church through the trees.'

'Rather you than me,' Liz said, with an exaggerated shiver. 'Better go and see what the children are up to.' She hurried out of the room and through the kitchen. Opening the back door, she called, 'Edward, Rosie, Amy, where are you?'

There was no sign of them but they could hear giggling and high, raised voices as the children called to one another.

'Come on, kids. We've got to go.' Liz took a step forward as Edward emerged through a gap in the hedge. There were leaves in his hair and a streak of mud on his cheek. 'Look at the state of you. What on earth have you been up to? And where are Rosie and Amy?'

'I don't know. We were playing hide and seek and I can't find them.' His face crumpled and he looked as if he was about to cry.

'Don't worry. Lucy's with them. And they can't have gone far,' Jo said. 'I'll go and look.'

As she started towards the gap in the hedge, Lucy appeared holding each of the girls by the hand. 'Here they are,' she said, smiling. 'We had a good game, didn't we?'

'Where did you hide then? I looked everywhere,' Edward said.

'Not telling,' said Rosie. 'It's a secret place. The other children showed us.'

'What children?' Liz asked.

Lucy shrugged. 'I didn't see them — just heard them playing in the churchyard.'

Liz turned to her sister, eyebrows raised in inquiry.

'I don't know,' Jo said. 'They must come from the houses further down the lane. I imagine the churchyard is an exciting place to play.'

'Well, I'm not keen on my kids playing there. I hope you get that gap in the hedge blocked up before they come to stay.'

'Don't worry. It will all be made safe by then. Plenty of time, anyway.'

'I suppose so.' Liz bent to brush the dirt and dead leaves off Rosie's jumper. 'Better get this lot home and in the bath. Right kids, in the car.'

As they drove away Liz looked back at the house and shuddered. 'Are you sure you're doing the right thing, Jo? It's a lot to take on.'

'Well I can't back out now! Besides, I've fallen in love with the place.'

It seemed that the girls felt the same.

'We love it too, don't we, Amy?' Rosie said.

'Yes. When can we come again?' Amy bounced in the seat.

Edward frowned. 'Well, I don't like it, Auntie Jo. It's so dark and gloomy. A bit scary … '

'Don't be so silly, Edward. It's just a house. When it's all done up it won't be so dark any more,' Jo said.

But as they turned out of the lane into the main road she had a moment of doubt. What was it about the New Rectory that caused such different reactions? She had felt drawn to it right from the first glimpse and the girls had enjoyed a happy couple of hours playing in the garden. But Liz and Edward obviously felt uncomfortable and wanted to get away as soon as possible. Lucy, too, had hated it at first, although now it seemed she was beginning to come round to the idea of living there.

5

When Jo arrived at work the following Monday, Clive was in the library sorting some papers.

'Good weekend?' he asked.

'Great. I've bought a house,' Jo said. She had already told him about the difficulties of finding the right property and he'd been sympathetic, although she felt he really didn't understand the problem. After all, he had come over from Canada to a property he already owned, albeit a dilapidated mausoleum of a place. But at least he had the money to make it habitable.

'Congratulations,' he said now. 'Where is it?'

'Only a little way from here. The lane just off the Winterbourne road, next door to St Mark's Church.' She paused, frowning. 'I'm not sure if I've done the right thing, actually.'

66

'But you wanted to be nearer here, didn't you?'

'That's the main reason I went for it, I suppose,' Jo said. 'I took my sister to see it the other day and she thinks I'm crazy.'

Clive grinned. 'Why's that then?'

'Well, it needs a lot of work doing. Everything, in fact. Kitchen, bathroom, roof ... '

'If you need any tradesmen, I can recommend those working here. I'm really pleased with what they've done so far.'

'Thanks. That's worth knowing. I hope to do some of it myself but I don't think I'm up to roofing or plumbing,' she said with a laugh.

Clive laughed too, then gave a little cough, pointing to the papers he had put on the desk.

'There's some interesting stuff there about the family history. Could you put it in some sort of order for me, please?'

It was a gentle hint that she should be getting on with her job and Joanne hastily nodded and sat down at the desk. She didn't mind at all. Clive usually left her to get on with things in her own time and wasn't forever looking over her shoulder. But he was so enthusiastic about his project that he couldn't wait to see results. And, in the few weeks since starting at the Manor she had caught his enthusiasm. The Grayling family was fascinating and a real story was beginning to emerge as she sorted and catalogued the mouldering old documents and ledgers. She still hadn't discovered how Clive's branch of the family had ended up in Canada, though.

$$\star \quad \star \quad \star$$

With her house already sold and the New Rectory standing empty, the sale had gone through quite quickly. Jo could sense the agent's relief at having got it off his hands at last. She had to admit there were a few more moments of doubt as to whether she had done the right thing. She wondered what horrors she would find once she started stripping wallpaper and ripping out fixtures.

She had decided to do the decorating

herself — she'd always done it in their old house and was quite competent with a paintbrush and wallpaper paste. She was handy with a screwdriver and electric drill too.

As soon as they moved in, she couldn't wait to get started. The roof was the main priority and she took Clive up on his offer to release the workmen from the Manor to get it done as soon as possible.

'Luckily we've had a good summer after all that rain. It's had a chance to dry out a bit,' Jo said.

'Yes. I can't believe how hot it's been lately,' Clive said with a laugh.

Joanne laughed too. 'That could change though. You don't know our English climate,' she said.

'Let's hope it lasts until you get the roof fixed. Once that's done, you'll be able to get on with inside and at least make it habitable.'

It hadn't been as bad as she'd feared; she had stripped off the peeling paper in the front room, deciding not to re-do it until the central heating was installed. The hot weather had continued but autumn was fast approaching. Already there was a chill in the air first thing in the mornings. The sun streamed in through the large bay window at the front of the house, so the room was usually pleasantly warm. But towards the back of the house, especially in the small room which Joanne had chosen as her study, there seemed to be a permanent chill. Lucy had also complained about the cold in her bedroom, which was directly over the study and she had moved to a smaller room at the front of the house.

Jo hoped the new heating system would rectify it and that there wasn't some serious underlying problem which would cost a lot to sort out. How did they manage with just open fires in those days? she wondered. It would be nice to have a log burner though, and there were all those trees at the end of the garden which could be cut back and burnt. After a day working in the chilly environment of the Manor's library, it would be good to come back to a cosy home.

It was a bit chaotic, working around the carpenters and tilers, who were now in the middle of fitting the new kitchen.

Lucy grumbled as she balanced a plate on her lap in the living room.

'It's like living on a building site,' she said.

'Well, we sort of are, really! It'll be lovely when it's finished though,' Jo said.

'When!' Lucy gave an exaggerated sigh.

'You'll be gone in a couple of weeks and by the time you come home at half term it'll all be finished. Meantime you'll just have to put up with the building site, won't you?'

Jo softened her remark with a little laugh and Lucy responded with a grin.

'I hate to admit it, Mum, but this house is growing on me. And I love the garden.'

'The jungle, you mean.'

'I'll have a go at clearing some of it, if you like, while you're at work tomorrow,' Lucy offered.

'You sure? You've such a lot to do before you go away.' Lucy would soon be off to Exeter University.

'I need a break from all that. It'll be fun. I'll get Ben to help.'

Joanne smiled and thanked her.

When Lucy had gone up to her room, Jo switched on her computer and opened up the spreadsheet showing the work to be done and the costs involved. Although she'd allowed some contingency, things were threatening to spiral out of control. She would have to modify some of her more ambitious plans for the house. The conservatory would definitely be put on hold for a while.

After a short session she rubbed her eyes and switched off the machine. She spent far too much time looking at screens these days, not to mention peering at faded old documents up at the Manor. At this rate she'd be needing glasses.

After a quick tidy up, she went upstairs, wishing she'd had the shower installed before embarking on the renovation of the kitchen. At the moment there was only a washbasin and toilet in the bathroom, the bath having been removed the previous day. Still, it would all be finished soon and she could begin to relax and enjoy her new home.

At least Lucy was beginning to be more positive about things.

She knocked on her daughter's bedroom door, tentatively opening it when there was no reply. Surely she wasn't asleep already. But the room was empty. Where was she?

It wasn't quite dark yet and Jo wondered if she'd gone out into the garden, although she couldn't imagine why. She crossed to the window and looked out, just in time to see Lucy disappearing through the gap in the hedge.

'What on earth?' she muttered. Had she planned to meet a boyfriend? Joanne thought the only lad she was interested was Ben, who was always welcome at the house. She shook her head. It wasn't like Lucy to be secretive.

Curious, she went downstairs and out of the back door. With all the work going on in the house she hadn't taken much interest in the garden so far and it was with some surprise that she noticed a well-trodden path through the waist-high weeds to the gap in the hedge. Had Lucy gone into the churchyard — and why, at this time of night? Joanne knew that she'd been intrigued by the ancient church but it was a bit late in the evening to be exploring.

Dusk was falling and Jo shivered as an owl hooted nearby. Sometimes she forgot that the New Rectory, for all its suburban look, was almost in the country. And despite the other houses further along the lane, it was quite isolated. She ducked through the gap, peering through the gloom and gasping as she caught a flash of white. Lucy, dressed only in her nightie, was bending over the graves of the small children which they had discovered on their first visit here. What was it about them that fascinated her so? Jo wondered.

She was about to call out but the words died on her lips as Lucy stood up and turned, a smile on her face. Then she raised her arms above her head and pirouetted in a circle, humming a tune. She held out her arms, laughing.

'Come on, dance,' she called.

For a moment Jo thought she was speaking to her but as she took a step forwards she realised that Lucy was unaware of her presence. Horrified yet somehow fascinated, she watched as her daughter danced around the gravestones, still humming that tune. She seemed to be in a trance and Joanne shivered. What was happening to the girl?

She didn't know how many minutes passed but she couldn't bear it any longer. She took a step forward and called out.

'Lucy, what are you doing?'

Startled, the girl looked round, her eyes wide and full of fear.

'Who is it? What do you want?' she whispered. Then her face cleared and she looked down at her bare feet, stained with grass, a puzzled frown on her face.

'Lucy, come indoors — now.' Jo's voice was sharp with anxiety.

Lucy seemed to notice her for the first time. 'Mum, what's going on?'

'I could ask you that,' Jo said. 'It's a bit late to be messing about out here, isn't it? What made you come outside, and in your nightie too?'

Lucy shook her head. 'I was looking out of the window. I thought I saw something.'

Jo decided not to mention her daughter's strange behaviour. It was as if Lucy had no memory of what she had been doing. Thank goodness she had realised the girl was no longer in her room. Who knew what might have happened if she had stayed out there any longer?

6

The next day Lucy came downstairs rubbing her eyes and yawning.

Jo looked at her anxiously. There were dark circles under her eyes and she looked tired.

'Didn't you sleep?' she asked.

Lucy shrugged. ''Course I did,' she said.

Jo herself had lain awake for hours wondering what to do about Lucy's actions the previous evening. Had she been sleep-walking? She was really worried. If only there was someone she could confide in.

Usually she would talk things over with her sister. But since her last visit, Liz had been feeling poorly. Her symptoms had worsened and her doctor was trying to get her into hospital a bit earlier. She had enough on her plate without Jo loading problems onto her.

Lucy was pouring cereal into a bowl while Jo made tea, stealing anxious glances at her daughter as she did so. But the girl seemed to have suffered no ill effects from her sojourn in the graveyard, apart from the shadows under her eyes. Then she began to hum under her breath and Jo gave a hastily suppressed gasp. That was the tune she'd been humming last night.

'Lucy, what's that you're humming?' she asked. 'It sounds familiar — like a nursery rhyme.'

'Don't know.' Lucy looked confused.

'Where did you pick it up?'

'It just popped into my head.' She laughed. 'Now I suppose I'll have it on my brain all day.'

She grabbed her iPod off the worktop and shoved the earbuds into place, turning the volume up high so that the sound leaked out into the room.

'There, that will get rid of it,' she said.

Jo winced but didn't comment. Her daughter's choice of music was a constant source of disagreement but today she was prepared to put up with it. Although the tune Lucy had been humming had sounded like a nursery rhyme, a half-remembered childhood memory, the sound had sent a shiver down her spine. There was something eerie about it but she couldn't quite put her finger on why she found it so disturbing.

She brought the mugs over to the table and sat down, her brow still wrinkled in thought. Why had Lucy gone to the graveyard so late? She'd said she thought she saw someone but why hadn't she called her mother. They could have investigated together. She shrugged and took a sip of her tea. Perhaps she'd been sleep-walking, but although she looked tired, she seemed all right, shovelling cereal into her mouth while jiggling in time to the music leaking from her iPod.

Lucy finished her breakfast and pushed her bowl away, turning to her mother and saying, 'Mum, do you believe in ghosts?'

'What? Don't be silly, of course I don't. What made you ask?'

'I don't know really. I was just thinking

about you working in that creepy old place.'

'It's not creepy at all. Why is it that old houses have to be haunted? You've been watching too many horror films.' Jo gave a little laugh but it was mingled with a sigh of relief that Lucy had been talking about the Manor, and not this house.

She shook her head and hastily finished her tea. Why had she been so quick to think Lucy was referring to the New Rectory? Was it because of her behaviour last night?

Joanne hastily dismissed the thought. The workmen would be here soon and it was time she was leaving for the Manor.

'Please will you do the washing up? I haven't time,' she asked, putting her cup in the washing up bowl.

'Can't it wait till the dishwasher's fitted?'

'I'd rather it was done now. I think they're coming to do it today, but just in case they don't, I don't want to come home to a sink full of dirty dishes.'

'But there's only the electric

80

kettle — it's such a pain. Bad enough not having a proper shower.'

'Lucy, do stop complaining. It's only for a couple more days. Clive is lending me some more of his workmen. They can't get on up at the Manor, they're waiting for materials.'

Lucy grinned. 'Clive, eh? What happened to 'Mr Grayling'? Getting friendly, aren't you.'

'Don't be silly, Lucy. He's my boss. They're not so formal where he comes from.' She picked up her bag and took her jacket off the back of the chair. 'So, what are you doing today?'

'I told you. I'm going to start on clearing the garden.'

'Are you sure you wouldn't rather be out with your friends? After all, you'll be off soon enough. Why not make the most of your time with them?' After last night's episode Jo was feeling uneasy at the thought of leaving Lucy alone in the house all day, anxious that she might be tempted to spend more time in the churchyard.

'It's OK. I'll get Ben to come over and help.'

'Good idea.' Jo was relieved. Ben Carter had been Lucy's escort at the end of term prom and they had spent quite a bit of time together since then. He was a nice lad and Jo had no qualms about him spending the day here. Besides, the workmen would be around too. That would take Lucy's mind off her obsession with the children's graves, she thought.

* * *

She got her bicycle out of the shed and started off along the track which ran behind the church. It had once been the main coach road from London and was now used by cyclists and walkers wanting to get out of town and enjoy the countryside. As she rode along, breathing in the scent of autumn leaves, she found she was humming the same tune Lucy had been humming.

'Ladybird, ladybird, fly away home,' she murmured as the words popped

82

into her head. Now why would she find that so disturbing? It was just an old nursery rhyme.

When she arrived at the Manor she was relieved that there was no sign of Clive. The worry over what was happening with Lucy had quenched the enthusiasm with which she usually greeted each day's work and she needed time to settle down and get her head round the tasks she had earmarked for today.

She hung her jacket up and went into the library, looking around at the vast array of documents, books, pamphlets and other papers that littered the huge room.

For the first time since starting the job, she felt a bit overwhelmed. She shook her head. No, she was just feeling unsettled, remembering the blank expression in her daughter's eyes as she danced round the gravestones in St Mark's churchyard. Hopefully it had just been a one-off incident, sleep-walking brought on by anxiety over the move as well as starting at university. At least by the time Jo had left for work Lucy had seemed her normal self, chatting on her mobile to Ben and giving a cheerful wave as Jo went out of the door.

Still, she would keep a close eye on her and, if it happened again, she would seek professional help. With a determined sigh, she pulled her chair up to the desk and switched on the computer.

She had already made a start on sorting the various documents into categories but now she decided that before she went any further she would set up the database to record details of the collection.

She had just brought up the spread-sheet when Clive came in carrying an armful of papers.

'Ah, Jo, just found these in the base-ment,' he said, lowering them onto the long table under the window. 'Lots of interesting stuff here.'

He glanced over her shoulder at the screen and she caught a faint hint of citrus aftershave. Quite pleasant, she thought, flushing a little as she remem-bered her daughter's teasing remark that morning. She thrust the thought away hastily and pushed her chair back.

'How are you getting on?' he asked.

'I'm not sure really,' she confessed. 'I'm worried I've taken on too much.'

'Nonsense. You're doing fine. And remember, you can take all the time you need. I realise this is a mammoth job. Most of this stuff hasn't been touched for years.'

Jo went over to the long table and pulled one of the sheets of parchment towards her, releasing a cloud of dust.

'I can tell,' she said with a laugh.

They pored over the document which was a list of materials and costs for repairs to one of estate buildings.

'Such lovely handwriting,' Jo commented.

'It's beautiful. Almost a work of art in itself,' Clive agreed. He pointed to the date at the top — 1890. 'The owner then was my great-grandfather, I think. He was doing a lot of improvements to the farm cottages and barns at that time.'

Jo felt a little jolt. That date rang a bell

somewhere. Perhaps it had been mentioned in one of the other documents, but she had read so much over the past few weeks she couldn't be expected to remember everything. Time to get started on that database, as well as the family tree Clive was so interested in, she thought.

There was a knock on the library door and a workman put his head round, saying, 'Problem, boss. Can you come and look?'

'Be with you in a minute,' Clive said, turning to Jo with a laugh. 'Now you know why you're here. I'd much rather be working on this stuff. But the house needs me.'

When he'd gone, Jo found herself smiling. Happy as she was to be left alone to concentrate on her work, she realised that she enjoyed these moments with Clive, talking about the project and his plans for the house. Not that she was attracted to him in the slightest, or so she told herself. It was their common interest in the history of the Manor and the Grayling family that made him such a congenial companion.

She pushed the thought away and got started on the database, first of all setting up a spreadsheet with boxes for the date, type of document and a brief resume of the contents.

She became so absorbed that when Clive returned carrying two mugs of coffee she was quite surprised at how much time had passed. And, she realised, until now she hadn't thought about Lucy and the strange events of the previous evening at all.

She pushed her chair back, rubbed her eyes and gratefully accepted the mug, smiling her thanks. Taking a sip, she said, 'I needed that.'

'I noticed,' Clive said with a grin. 'You were so wrapped up in what you were doing, you didn't even hear me come in.'

'I'm finding it all so fascinating,' she replied.

'I must say it's a treat to have found someone who is so interested in their work. You're not at all like the picture I had in my head of a librarian.'

'The kind of librarian you were thinking of is a bit of a cliché,' Jo said, smiling to take the edge off her remark.

He grinned. 'You got me. I guess my ideas are a little old-fashioned. Things have moved on while I was growing up in the wilds of Canada.'

★　★　★

Jo wheeled her bike into the shed and looked at her watch. Home in less than five minutes, she thought. A far cry from the stressful drive she used to have to do, from the college library to her old house. How had she managed that for so many years? Apart from the niggling worry about her daughter, her life had certainly changed for the better since moving to the New Rectory. All she needed now was for the workmen to have finished the kitchen and started on the bathroom.

She walked round the side of the house, noting with pleasure that Lucy and Ben had cleared much of the overgrown vegetation which had obscured the end of the garden. The plot looked much bigger now and Joanne was looking forward to future planning and planting. It'll have to wait till the spring though, she thought. Getting the house sorted for the winter was priority.

When she went indoors Lucy was sitting at the kitchen table cradling a mug of coffee.

'Hi, Mum. Good day?' she asked.

'Busy but interesting,' Jo replied with a smile, pleased to see that no trace of Lucy's night-time wanderings remained. The shadows had disappeared and her eyes were sparkling.

'I've been busy too,' Lucy said.

'I noticed. Well done. You and Ben must have worked hard.'

'Ben didn't turn up. Jack helped.' Lucy waved a hand towards the young man who was lounging against the kitchen worktop, a mug in his hand.

'Glad to be of service, Mrs Mason.'

Startled, Jo turned to see that the figure she'd taken to be Lucy's boyfriend was one of the kitchen fitters.

'I thought you were supposed to be working on my kitchen.' Jo's voice was sharper than she'd intended but she was unreasonably annoyed at his lazy grin and the familiar way he leaned against the worktop.

'Mum!' Lucy protested. 'Jack stayed behind after he'd finished work. The others left at four o'clock.'

'That was kind of you,' Jo said, somewhat mollified when the young man pointed out that the job was almost finished.

'You've got your hot water and the dishwasher's plumbed in. Just the cosmetic bits to do now. It'll be all done by the time you get home tomorrow, then we can make a start on your shower,' he said. He finished his drink and rinsed the cup under the tap. 'Better be getting off then. See you tomorrow,' he said, winking at Lucy.

When he'd gone Jo was tempted to warn Lucy against getting too friendly with the workmen but she didn't want to be accused of snobbery. But it wasn't that. There was something about Jack Wilson that made her uneasy and she didn't like the thought of her daughter being alone in the house with him. She bit her tongue and kept quiet, instead asking if Lucy wanted anything to eat.

As she prepared a meal, enjoying working in the almost completed kitchen, she chatted about the work she'd been doing up at the Manor.

'You're really loving it, aren't you, Mum?' Lucy said as they sat down to plates of spaghetti bolognese.

'I am. I'm just beginning to realise how bored I was with my old job. It was time for a change.'

'New house, new job ... It's all change isn't it, Mum?' Lucy's voice was a little sad and Joanne knew she was thinking of her father. She still missed Tom too but they had to move on.

'It's all change for you too, love. You'll be moving away soon. A whole new life. An exciting life too — meeting new people, making new friends.'

'I'll miss my old friends, but you're

right, Mum. And I have to admit I've come to accept the house and everything. I hated the idea of moving, as you know, but now we're knocking this place into shape, I'll look forward to coming home in the holidays.'

As they talked about Lucy's plans for the future, Jo put the encounter with the young workman to the back of her mind. Perhaps she had imagined that little spark she thought she'd detected between Jack and her daughter. She hoped so.

7

Lucy was looking more like her old self and Jo hoped that the sparkle in her eyes was not down to the young kitchen fitter. Although she had no grounds for her distrust, she didn't want her daughter to get too friendly with him.

She was just getting ready to leave for work when there was a knock at the kitchen door. She was pleased that the workmen were early for a change — perhaps they would finish off the kitchen and move on to another job. The less time Jack spent at the New Rectory the better as far as she was concerned.

Lucy rushed to open the door.

'Hello, Ben. Glad you could make it today.'

Jo greeted him warmly. 'How nice to see you again, Ben. Don't let Lucy work you too hard.'

He laughed. 'Don't worry — I don't let her boss me around.'

'You saying I'm bossy?' Lucy giggled and slapped him on the shoulder.

Jo left them to their banter. Thank goodness she was behaving more like a normal teenager today, she thought.

But as she got her bicycle out, the workmen's van pulled up. Jack and his colleagues got out and all her misgivings returned. She couldn't explain, even to herself, why the sight of him sent a chill through her, so how could she warn her daughter not to get involved with him? She comforted herself with the thought that with Ben there, nothing untoward could happen.

When she got to the Manor, Clive was up a ladder, pulling back the ivy which climbed over the front porch, almost obscuring the carving over the lintel.

'Making the most of the fine weather to get some outside work done,' he said.

From the pile of vegetation on the ground, Jo could see that he'd been at it for some time.

'I expect you're ready for a coffee,' she said.

'Good idea. Give me ten minutes.'

She waved and went into the building, grinning at the thought of what Lucy would say. *'Making coffee for the boss — what are you, Mum? A slave?'*

She didn't really mind though. In fact, she was starting to look forward to their coffee breaks, when Clive would perch on the edge of her desk and talk about the project and his plans for the future.

The repairs to the Manor were coming along fast and every day saw an army of workmen swarming over the roof, up in the attics and down in the cellars. Clive was doing much of the work himself — he was very much an outdoors man, as Jo had thought, in spite of his interest in old manuscripts and ledgers.

In that way he was very like her late husband, and Jo wondered if that was why she enjoyed spending time with him. But he wasn't Tom, was he? No one could replace the man she had fallen in love with as a teenager, and who remained the love of her life.

Her brooding thoughts were interrupted when Clive came into the makeshift kitchen where she was waiting for the kettle to boil.

'Everything all right, Jo?' he asked.

She nodded and poured the water into the mugs.

'How's the work on the house coming along?'

'Good. The kitchen's nearly done. Thanks to your men, we've got hot water now — and they're going to put the new shower and bath in tomorrow.'

Clive laughed. 'That's more than I have. Still, the new materials will be delivered soon and they can get on with this.'

'I suppose a few kitchen units from Homebase wouldn't do?'

'Hardly. This is a listed building, which is causing all sorts of problems. I have to use materials which are 'in keeping', whatever that means.'

'It'll be worth it when it's all done though,' Jo said. 'It was very kind of you to lend me your men. Everyone was booked up and I would have had to wait ages.'

'No problem. It's not like they can get anything done in here at the moment anyway. It's good that they've got something to keep them occupied. As for me, after years of roughing it out on the oil fields, this place is a palace. But I guess a teenager can't live without her shower and mod cons.' He finished his coffee and got up.

'Better get on,' he said.

Jo nodded and switched on the computer.

At the door, Clive turned back and said, 'Nothing worrying you is there?'

'Not really.'

'There is, I can tell. Is it Lucy?'

'Just the usual teenage problems,' she said with a little laugh.

Clive smiled. 'Can't help you there, I'm afraid. She's not getting in with the wrong crowd, is she?'

'Nothing like that.' She shook her head. 'It's just with her going off to uni so soon … I'll miss her. Even her strops!'

When he'd gone, Jo couldn't settle to the job with her usual enthusiasm. She kept seeing in her mind's eye Jack's easy familiarity, that smarmy grin on his face. Please, Lucy, don't be taken in by him, she prayed silently.

She straightened her shoulders and resolutely put him out of her head. But perhaps she would have a word with Clive. He might know something of the young man's background and could put her mind at rest. She couldn't fault his work or that of the other tradesmen; it was his personality that troubled her.

★   ★   ★

Once she got stuck into cataloguing the latest batch of documents that Clive had found in a trunk in the attic her worries faded as once more she found herself caught up in the history of the Grayling family.

She pushed her chair back and stood up, rubbing the back of her neck. Time for a break after so long staring at the computer. She walked over to the long table under the window, where Clive had placed a box of old photographs.

She flicked through them, noting that many of them were spotted with mildew; some were even stuck together. She separated them out carefully, trying not to damage them even further, and spread them out on the table under the window. Perhaps it would be possible to restore them. It could probably be done on the computer, but it was beyond her expertise. She would ask Clive if he knew of anyone who could do it. It would be a shame if these precious records of the house and its previous generations were lost.

She smiled at the stiff, formal poses of earlier Graylings in their dark clothes, the men with their high collars and waistcoats with watch and chain; the women in their tightly-corseted bodices. Who were these people? she wondered, turning one group portrait over in case there were names written on the back. No luck. Was there any way she could find out who they were? Perhaps there would be a clue in the letters she was cataloguing.

Intrigued, she picked up another which showed a portrait of a striking young woman with dark hair piled on top of her head. A few stray curls framed her cheeks and she stared out of the photo with a calm direct gaze. She was dressed in a high-necked, tight-fitting bodice decorated with what looked like jet beads. Turning the picture over, she made out the faintly pencilled words, 'Sophie Blandford'. A shiver ran down her back and she looked round to see if the door had opened. But there was nobody there.

Shrugging, she put the photo down and picked up the next one, giving a little gasp. It showed a large Jacobean villa set back from the road in a large garden. There were two bay windows with leaded lights on either side of a wide porch and, on one corner, a square tower with a pointed roof. A row of small windows were obviously attics. The edges of the photo were blurred with damp but there was something written at the bottom.

She took it over to the window for a closer look, her eyes widening in disbelief as she made out the words, 'St Mark's Rectory'.

'It's my house,' she murmured. Well, not really, she amended in her head. For a start it was much bigger than the present-day building. This must be the house that had burnt down. But why was a photo of it in among mementoes of Clive's family? What connection could the Rectory possibly have with Grayling Manor? She must find out.

A shiver ran down her back and she had a feeling that it might be better to leave well alone. But it was too much of a coincidence to be ignored.

She put the photograph on one side and carried on sorting out the rest but she couldn't get the picture of the Rectory out of her head. From time to time she picked it up and stared at it as if she could penetrate the mystery. What connection was there with the Grayling family?

She thought of going in search of Clive to ask if he knew anything about it but he didn't like to be interrupted at his work, especially if he was up a ladder or unloading materials from a delivery lorry. It would have to wait till lunch time, she decided.

Cataloguing the photos and adding them to the database was not as interesting as examining the documents themselves but the time passed quickly and she was surprised when she heard the big clock in the Great Hall chiming twelve.

She stood up and stretched. She'd go and make a drink and hope that Clive was taking a break too. But before leaving the library she couldn't resist picking up the mystery photo again.

She ran her finger over it, removing a film of dust. The top left-hand corner was foxed with damp but she could make out the shadowy form of the church in the background. She could just imagine a large Victorian family living there.

'Definitely my house,' she muttered, 'or at least the one that was there before.' She shivered a little and the photo trembled in her hand. There was something about the house, a feeling of déjà vu. She shook her head.

'Don't be so silly,' she muttered. It was just that she had recognised it, she told herself.

She hastily put the print down and went into the kitchen, disappointed that Clive wasn't there. She had hoped for a chance to ask him about the photo.

While she waited for the kettle to boil she looked around the huge kitchen with its vaulted ceiling and mullioned windows, trying to imagine what it would look like when it was re-fitted. She had seen the plans and she pictured it looking something like the old kitchens in National Trust houses. What a pity so much of the original furniture had been lost, she thought. All that remained was the stone sink in the corner and an oak table which now held the electric kettle and a few mugs.

She made her coffee and got her sandwiches out of her bag. Usually she went for a walk in the grounds during her lunch break but today she wanted to get back to the photographs.

Carrying her mug, she entered the library, and was soon so immersed in work that she forgot to eat or drink. She didn't even realise Clive had come in until he spoke, making her jump.

'Making progress?' he asked.

'Not as much as I'd have liked,' she said. 'So many of these pictures are practically ruined with the damp.'

'I don't suppose many of them are worth keeping,' he said, picking one of them up and holding it up to the light from the window. 'Still, we could see about getting some of the more interesting ones restored. We could display them when we open to the public.'

'That's what I thought,' Joanne said. 'It would be a shame to lose any of them though.' She wondered whether to mention the stray picture she had discovered, but it was doubtful if Clive could shed any light on it. She decided to keep quiet until she had done a little more research.

He left her to it and she eagerly turned

to the pile of papers again. But as she worked through them she could find no reference to St. Mark's Rectory and she decided that it was a mystery that might never be solved. If she hadn't been living in the house which had replaced the original she would probably not have taken much notice of the picture.

'Oh, well,' she muttered, 'I'll just have to concentrate on the Manor. There's enough interesting history here without me making up mysteries.'

By the end of the afternoon she had made considerable headway and the database was growing. The information it contained, aside from being a record of what the house contained, would be invaluable when it came to compiling the guidebook.

She had switched off the computer and was tidying her desk when her hand fell on the photograph of St. Mark's Rectory. On impulse, she picked it up and slipped it into her bag.

She was about to leave when Clive returned, his hair and clothes wreathed in cobwebs and covered in dust.

'What happened to you?' she asked, laughing. But the laugh died when she saw that he was limping.

'Whatever you do, don't go up in the attics in the west wing,' he said, his voice hoarse with the dust he'd inhaled. 'I knew it was dangerous. Dry rot. I was rummaging around and put my foot through a floorboard. Should have been more careful. Twisted my ankle.'

'Are you OK?' Jo helped him into a chair, noticing streaks of blood running down his arm.

'I'm fine,' he said, stifling a cough.

'No, you're not. I'll go and get some water.'

She hurried into the kitchen at the end of the long passage, her heart thumping. Suppose he'd been badly hurt? In this huge house no one would have heard him cry out for help and he could have lain there all night. She would not have thought to go in search of him to say goodbye, as she usually left a note on her desk if there was anything he needed to know.

It was as she was wetting a cloth under the tap that she realised her concern for Clive Grayling was more than that of just an employee.

She tried to ignore the feeling and rushed back to the library. Clive was still sitting where she'd left him, his head in his hands. She made him drink some water and then proceeded to bathe the cut on his arm. Once it was cleaned she saw that it had looked worse than it was, but he still appeared badly shaken.

'Let me look at that ankle,' she said.

'It feels better now. Look, no swelling.' He stuck his foot out. 'I thought I was going to fall right through the floor,' he said. 'Luckily I managed to pull myself up. That's how I hurt my arm.' He looked up at her and took her hand. 'Thank goodness you were still here. I thought you'd gone home.'

The touch of his hand sent a jolt through her and, to hide her confusion, she pulled away and searched for paracetamol in her bag.

'Take a couple of these,' she said, 'and I should go and lie down if I were you. You'll feel better in the morning.'

'Can you stay a while, Jo — please?' he said, reaching for her hand again.

'I really ought to get home. You'll be all right, I'm sure, but call me if you need anything,' she said, striving to keep her voice even.

He tried to smile. 'Sure I will,' he said, getting up from the chair.

Joanne gathered up her coat and bag.

'I'll say goodbye, then. And no more rummaging around in attics without letting someone know what you're up to.'

'Yes, Ma'am,' he said.

Confident that he seemed to have recovered and would be all right if left on his own, Jo hurried outside. But, as she set off home, she could still feel the pressure of his hand on hers. Had she imagined it, as well as that pleading look in his eyes when he'd asked her to stay? She couldn't deny that she had very much wanted to say 'yes'.

Could she be falling in love with her

boss, the very thing she had vowed would not happen when she had accepted the job at Grayling Manor?

8

1890

If only there was someone I could confide in, Sophie thought. She certainly couldn't speak to her husband. The Reverend Thomas Blandford was a good man, adept at sorting out the various problems of the villagers, but he was very strait-laced. The slightest hint of immorality would shock him beyond measure. Not that Sophie really thought there was anything immoral going on. But she was worried about her brother. Surely it was just an innocent flirtation? That wasn't how Thomas would see it though.

Perhaps she was being foolish, she thought, glancing out of the window and smiling. The children were shrieking with laughter as Philip chased them round the garden. Her younger brother was still such a child himself, she thought indulgently. But the smile faded when Margaret, the children's nursemaid, came out carrying a pitcher of lemonade and five glasses.

Philip came to an abrupt halt at the sight of the girl and, even at this distance, Sophie could see the look on his face. It was clear he was smitten with the pretty nursemaid and she, returning the look, obviously felt the same.

Sophie tried to stifle her feeling of foreboding. As long as neither of them did anything about it, all would be well, she thought. But Philip had spent far too much time here while on vacation, time he should have been spending with Alice, to whom he had been betrothed almost from childhood. She was the daughter of Sir Sidney Blake, a local wealthy land-owner. It would be a good match for the younger son of the Grayling family. Surely Philip must realise that even a minor dalliance could well cause Sir Sidney to insist that his daughter broke off her engagement. Thank goodness Philip was due to return to Oxford soon.

But this was no flirtation — it was much more serious, Sophie realised as she watched the young couple. Margaret had poured lemonade for the children, who were now sitting quietly on the grass under the elm tree. She passed a glass to Philip and before she could let go he had grasped her hand and leaned forward, whispering something in her ear. She flushed and tried to pull away, but at the same time she was smiling. She glanced towards the house and Sophie thought she was protesting. But Philip laughed and shook his head, seemingly careless of their being observed.

Thank goodness Thomas was out visiting sick parishioners, Sophie thought. She knew that if he had the slightest suspicion anything untoward was going on, he would dismiss Margaret on the spot. And I can't lose her, Sophie thought. She's so good with the children. I couldn't possibly train anyone to do the job half as well. Besides, the children love her. They'd be devastated if she left them.

Sophie felt a spasm of pity for her

brother. She knew what it was like to fall in love with someone deemed unsuitable for anyone of their station in life. But that was all in the past. She was happy — or at least, content — with Thomas, and more than happy with her home and her children.

She let her mind drift back to that last encounter with Richard, the handsome young sculptor who had been employed at Grayling Manor. 'Yes, Richard, I do love you,' she had said. 'But don't you see? It's impossible.'

'If you really loved me, you wouldn't hesitate,' he said.

'But, Richard — running away with you? Let me speak to Father. I'm sure he'll come round in the end.'

'He won't. You know very well, he won't. This is the only way.'

Yes, she had been tempted, but the fear of her family's wrath, the shame and disgrace had proved too much. She had been very young and foolish at the time, but even so, she had known that any future with Richard was just a dream. Even after all these years, though, she still thought of him more often than she should.

With a sigh, she tried to push the memories aside. But however hard she tried she would never forget the long, hot summer that Richard had spent creating the wonderful stone figures that supported the fountain in the middle of the great lawn at Grayling Manor. Whenever she could slip away from her governess, she would sneak out to the old barn where he had set up his workshop and watch him at work, mesmerised by his tanned, lean body and rippling muscles as he chiselled away at the hard stone.

When the work was completed she knew that Richard would have to leave. He had been commissioned to create a sculpture for one of Father's friends, whose stately home was at the other end of the country. When it was time to go, he had tried once more to persuade her to leave with him but she had held firm.

'Perhaps it's for the best,' he had said, giving her one last, tender kiss.

Remembering that kiss, Sophie ran her

finger over her lips, then shrugged and opened the French windows. She had done her duty, behaved as was expected of her and she could not say now that she was really unhappy with her situation. She was sure that Philip would feel the same in time — that's if he didn't do anything silly first.

She called out to the children to come in.

'Edward, Amelia, Rosalind — time for tea.'

The children reluctantly got to their feet and came indoors.

'Can't we play a bit longer?' Amelia said. 'Uncle Philip was telling us stories.'

'I'm sure your uncle has better things to do with his time,' Sophie said.

'I can think of nothing better than spending time with my nephew and nieces,' Philip said. But his eyes were on Margaret.

'Well, their father will be home soon and I want them all clean and tidy and ready to recite their lessons to him. Margaret, take them upstairs and see that they wash thoroughly. And change Rosalind's dress — that one has grass stains all down the back.' Sophie hated playing the stern matriarch but Thomas had very exacting standards and she was determined to live up to them. It might help to assuage the guilty thoughts she'd been having about Richard, she thought ruefully.

When the nursemaid had ushered the children upstairs, she turned to her brother.

'Philip ... '

'Don't, Sophie. I know what you're going to say. But I can't help it. I love her — and she loves me.'

'But there's no future in it, Philip. You'll never be allowed to marry. And what about Alice?'

Philip pulled a face. 'Alice doesn't love me. You know it is more of a business arrangement.'

'Philip, it can't go on. For one thing, if Thomas finds out he will dismiss Margaret without a reference.' She sighed. 'It's a good thing you're going back to

Oxford in a week or two. It will give you time to come to your senses.'

'I might not go back,' Philip muttered, his voice like a sulky child's.

'Don't talk such nonsense.'

'You don't understand … '

'I understand more than you think. I was young once, you know.' She gently touched his arm. 'The children will be down soon. Just say goodbye to them and go.'

'I thought I could stay for tea.'

'No, Philip. I think it's best if you leave now and stay away for a while. Give yourself time to think things over.'

There was no chance for him to reply as the children erupted into the room, their faces shiny from soap and water, Edward's hair slicked down and Rosalind pretty in her fresh muslin frock.

'I'm just off home. Come and give us a kiss,' Philip said, pasting a smile on his face.

'Must you go?' Amelia asked. 'You said you would put up a swing in the sycamore tree.'

'And I will, just not today.'

'Tomorrow, then?'

'Of course,' Philip said, raising his eyebrows at Sophie.

She nodded. 'All right. Come back tomorrow afternoon. The children have their lessons in the morning.'

'Goodbye, my lambs. See you tomorrow,' Philip said, kissing the girls. He turned to Edward and shook his hand in a very grown-up way, much to the little boy's delight.

The door opened and he looked around, his face reddening.

'I must go,' he said, rushing out of the room just as Margaret came in.

'I thought your brother was staying for tea, Ma'am,' the nursemaid said.

'He has another engagement. His fiancée is coming to dinner,' Sophie said.

Margaret flushed and turned away.

'Tea time, children,' she said, ushering them upstairs to the nursery.

Sophie heard the catch in the girl's voice and couldn't help feeling sorry for her. Perhaps she had been a bit harsh, mentioning Alice, but it did no harm to remind her that Philip was already spoken for.

She'd had to learn herself that duty came before desire and Margaret and her brother would have to learn that hard lesson too. She glanced out of the window as Philip mounted his horse and rode away across the fields in the direction of the manor.

She could not stop her brother from visiting and she prayed that nothing untoward would happen in the next two weeks. The sooner he was safely settled back at university the better — for all of them, she thought.

★   ★   ★

Thomas came into the nursery and looked approvingly at his children seated around the table, writing busily. Sophie was leaning over Rosalind's shoulder helping her to spell a word but she looked up with a smile as her husband came in.

'What good children,' he said. 'Come,

Edward, show me your work.'

The little boy passed his book across to his father and waited with bated breath as Thomas slowly ran his eye down the page of neat lettering.

'Very good, son. Now, Amelia, what about you?'

As he nodded approval there were sighs of relief all round and Sophie said, 'Well done, children. Now, go and wash your hands. It's nearly time for luncheon and afterwards you may go out to play.'

'Goody,' Rosalind said. 'Uncle Philip's coming later. He's going to put up a swing.'

The children got down from the table and left the room. As Sophie made to follow them, Thomas said, 'Your brother spends a lot of time here. I thought he'd be busy preparing to go back to Oxford.' A frown of disapproval furrowed his forehead.

'He tells me he's all packed and ready. You know how he loves the children. There won't be many more opportunities for him to play with them before he returns to his studies,' Sophie said.

As usual Thomas could not resist quoting the Bible.

"When I became a man I put away childish things.' Let's hope Philip has managed to grow up a bit while he's been at university. After all, when he comes down next year, he will be expected to take up a career.'

Sophie did not reply, knowing it was useless to try and defend her brother.

'Goodness knows what Alice thinks of his rampaging round the garden playing games when he should be applying himself to his studies,' her husband continued.

Privately, Sophie wished Thomas was more like her brother and would take time to play with his children rather than only talking to them about duty and obedience.

When her husband had gone downstairs to his study, telling her to call him when luncheon was served, she paused by the bathroom door, where Margaret was supervising the children's washing.

Rosalind, as usual, was chatting brightly, excited by the prospect of her uncle's visit later on.

Sophie's heart sank when she heard her daughter say, 'You like Uncle Philip, don't you, Margaret?'

'Yes, I do,' Margaret said.

'I wish he didn't have to go away. I'll miss him. I expect you will too, won't you.'

'I will.'

Sophie heard the catch in the nurse-maid's voice and she stepped into the room, forcing herself to speak calmly.

'Rosalind, stop chattering and finish washing your hands. And Margaret, go downstairs and see if Ruby has laid the table.'

Margaret's face was flushed and she barely murmured assent before rushing out of the room.

I must speak to her, Sophie thought. This must stop. It won't be long before Thomas realises what's going on. He'll dismiss Margaret and probably forbid Philip to visit as well.

When they had finished their meal, Thomas retired to his study to write his sermon, saying he did not wish to be disturbed. 'That means no playing under my window when you're outside,' he told the children. 'I can't concentrate when you're running about shouting.'

'We'll be good, Father,' Amelia said. 'Anyway, we'll be right down the end of the garden near the stable. Uncle Philip's going to make a swing in the sycamore tree.'

Thomas looked hard at Sophie. 'Do you think that's a good idea? One of them could get hurt.'

'I'm sure Philip will make sure it's safe,' Sophie said. 'You just get on with your sermon, dear, and stop worrying.'

'Very well, my dear. I'm sure you know best.'

Sophie bit her lip as she detected a trace of sarcasm in his voice. She would have to make sure that Philip did not allow the children to become too boisterous.

When Philip arrived, Sophie leaned

forward to kiss his cheek, saying, 'Thomas is busy writing his sermon. He needs peace and quiet so I am relying on you to keep the children occupied in the garden. It's a lovely day, so make the most of this sunshine.'

'Very well, Sophie. I'm sure we'll have a lovely time.'

The children had heard him arrive and they came down the stairs in a tumble of arms and legs.

'Uncle Philip, you haven't forgotten the swing?'

'Shh, children. Don't disturb your father,' Sophie admonished. She noticed Philip's eyes going to the top of the stairs in search of Margaret and shook her head. 'You must keep the children entertained this afternoon. I have given Margaret leave to go and visit her mother in the village. She has been rather poorly.'

Amelia tugged at Philip's hand. 'Come on, Uncle — the swing.'

Trying to hide his look of disappointment, Philip hoisted the little girl up onto his shoulder. 'All right, I'm coming.'

Sophie watched them from the French windows, smiling at the children's enjoyment of their uncle's company. He was so good with them and would make a wonderful father when the time came. She was sure that once he and Alice were married he would soon settle down and forget about Margaret. But even as she thought it, she knew she was deceiving herself.

She sighed and turned away, picking up her embroidery and trying to concentrate on the altar cloth she was making for the church. But after a few moments she threw it down and her eyes strayed to the window once more. She could not help a feeling of foreboding. Although Thomas appeared to be wrapped up in his calling, concentrating on his duties to his parishioners, he was bound to notice something eventually.

Philip was due to join the army when he came down from Oxford and Sophie knew it would be for the best. A separation would relieve both the young people of temptation. But he had confided that he preferred to stay at home and help his older brother to run the estate. Robert had been in poor health since a bout of pneumonia the previous winter and their father was only too pleased that Philip had started to show an interest.

If only he knew, Sophie thought. Her younger brother's only interest lay in staying at home to be near Margaret. Did he really think he could break his engagement to Alice and talk their father into allowing him to marry a lowly nursemaid?

She stood up with an impatient sigh. 'I must try and talk some sense into him,' she murmured, just as the door opened.

'What did you say, my dear?' Thomas asked.

'Oh, you startled me. I was just thinking that it was time for tea.'

'Excellent.' Thomas rubbed his hands and moved towards the fire.

'Have you finished your sermon?' Sophie asked.

'Just about. A few finishing touches needed. I'll work on it again after supper.'

Sophie rang the bell and Ruby came in a moment later with the tea tray.

'Shall I call Master Philip in, Ma'am?' the maid asked.

'Not yet, Ruby,' Sophie said. 'He seems to be enjoying himself out there with the children and they do love having him play with them.'

Ruby dropped a curtsey and left the room as Sophie poured the tea.

'Where is Margaret?' Thomas asked, settling himself in his favourite chair by the fire and reaching out for his cup and saucer.

'I know it's not her usual afternoon off, but she received a message that her mother was poorly so I gave her leave to visit for a few hours.'

'That was good of you, my dear. But don't let her take advantage of your kind heart. I fear she is becoming a little over-familiar. I saw her laughing and joking with your brother the other day — most unbecoming behaviour in a servant.'

'I'm sure she meant no harm,' Sophie

said quickly, with a nervous smile.

'Well, it's your job to manage the servants. I'm sure you will make sure there is no impropriety.' He finished his tea and stood up. 'I'll just take a turn in the garden, my dear. See what those children are up to.'

Sophie stood too as if to accompany him.

'No, my dear. You stay here. I need to have a word with my brother-in-law.'

Sophie's heart sank. Following on so quickly from his query as to Margaret's whereabouts, she was sure he had noticed the couple's infatuation with each other and was about to lecture Philip on the impropriety of a relationship with the nursemaid.

After a brief hesitation, she followed her husband outside and hurried down the path to the stables.

Philip had finished putting up the swing and she heard Amelia's high-pitched giggles as Edward pushed her.

Her brother was in earnest conversation with Thomas and she was just in time to hear him say, 'I can assure you, sir ... '

She put her hand to her mouth and stepped towards them, ready to intervene, then sighed with relief as Philip continued, ' ... it is perfectly safe.'

Amelia jumped off the swing and ran towards her father. 'Isn't Uncle Philip clever, Father?'

'Yes, my dear, very.' Thomas patted her head. 'Now, run along indoors, children.'

Reluctantly, they obeyed and Sophie and Philip accompanied them back to the house. Before following them, Thomas went over to the sycamore tree and pulled heavily on the rope fixing the swing to the sturdy branch. Satisfied, he caught up with his wife and her brother.

'Back to Oxford soon, then?' he said, clapping Philip on the shoulder. 'Your last year — make the most of it. Then it's time to get out in the real world. Army, isn't it?'

'I haven't decided yet, sir.'

'Nonsense. You've been offered a commission in your uncle's old regiment, haven't you?'

Philip didn't reply and Sophie gave a quick shake of her head. She hadn't mentioned her brother's change of plans to Thomas, knowing it would provoke a lecture from him.

'Are you staying for supper, Philip?' she asked, to fill the awkward moment.

'Can't, I'm afraid. The Blakes are coming over — a farewell dinner before I go away again.' He didn't sound very enthusiastic at the prospect of seeing his fiancée.

'We'll see you before you go though, won't we?'

Philip nodded.

As he was about to leave after saying goodbye to the children, he said, 'I do hope Margaret's mother is better soon.'

Thomas gave a short laugh. 'It's my belief the girl's mother is perfectly all right. She just wanted an excuse to go into the village. There is a young man there who is sweet on her, so I've heard. Joe, the blacksmith's apprentice.' He turned to his wife. 'It looks as if you might be looking for a new nursemaid before too long, my dear.'

'I'm sure you're wrong, Thomas. She would have told me.'

Sophie pretended she had not noticed Philip's stricken look, the blanching of his cheeks. She touched his arm, but before she could say anything else, he had grabbed his hat and rushed out of the house.

She watched him mount his horse and gallop off down the lane, digging the spurs into the poor animal's flanks.

As she supervised the children's supper, she resolved to question Margaret on her return. If she did have a beau in the village, perhaps she had merely been flirting with Philip. It should have been a relief, but something told her she was wrong. There was a real passion between her brother and the maid. Sophie could not suppress a sense of foreboding.

9

As Jo had feared, when she got home it was to find Jack in the kitchen with Lucy, and no sign of Ben. The two of them were laughing but they stopped abruptly when she came in.

She put her bag on the table and asked brightly, 'Ben gone home then?'

'He didn't stay long,' Lucy said, turning to Jack with a broad smile. 'We didn't miss him though, did we, Jack?'

Jo thought it best to ignore the innuendo in her daughter's voice and asked, 'What have you been up to then?'

'We've been busy, Mrs Mason — as you can see.' Jack pointed to the finished cupboards and tiling round the sink. 'We worked like mad to get it finished. Lucy helped too. We were all done by lunchtime.'

So why are you still here then? Jo thought.

But before she could say anything, Lucy said, 'Jack stayed behind to help cut back some more of the jungle.'

'That was kind of him.' She hoped her daughter hadn't noticed the edge to her voice.

'And, guess what — we found something interesting.' She grabbed Jo's arm. 'Come on, we'll show you.'

Jo let herself be propelled out of the back door and round the side of the house furthest away from the church. When she'd left for work that morning the stretch of ground between the hedge and the house had still been waist-high in weeds. The young people must have worked hard to clear it, revealing a patch of uneven soil, and something else.

'What is it?' she asked, poking at ground with her foot.

'Bricks. It looks like there was a building here at one time,' Lucy said, pointing.

A shiver went down Jo's back as she bent to brush away the dirt, exposing a stretch of broken brickwork. Were these part of the foundations of the old house?

She remembered the photo in her hand-bag but she was reluctant to show it to Lucy with Jack there.

'We'll have to get all this cleared away if we want to lay a lawn here,' she said matter-of-factly.

'Oh, no, we must leave it, at least for the time being,' Lucy said. 'It's part of the house's history. Jack and I want to do a proper excavation. It looks as if these bricks are really old.'

Lucy had always been interested in history. Even when she was quite small, when Jo and Tom had taken her to visit castles and stately homes she had always asked about the people who lived there. Now though, Jo felt a bit apprehensive, fearing what they might discover. It was an irrational fear, she knew, but she couldn't help feeling that they shouldn't be delving into the past. She tried to shake it off, giving a little laugh.

'Well, I'm not having that *Time Team* lot tramping all over my garden,' she said.

Jack had picked up a stick and was poking around in the undergrowth alongside the hedge. He seemed to sense Jo's feelings and said, 'No need for that, Mrs Mason.' He threw down the stick. 'Lucy, why don't we do some research in the library? They might have something about the old houses in the area.'

'Good idea.' She turned to her mother. 'Didn't that estate agent say there used to be a bigger house here? He said it burnt down.'

Joanne felt that shiver down her back again. It wasn't really cold out, but it was starting to get dark and she persuaded the young people to go inside.

'We can't do anything more now. Let's have another look at the weekend,' she suggested.

Once inside, she felt she ought to offer Jack a drink, but to her relief, he said he had to go.

He turned as Lucy was seeing him out.

'I'll see you tomorrow, Mrs Mason,' he said. 'I'm back at the Manor. The materials are being delivered tomorrow so I'll have to get on with Mr Grayling's kitchen now. One of the other lads is going to be doing your shower.'

Kissing Lucy's cheek, he said, 'Later?'

She nodded and closed the door.

'What was that all about? I thought Ben was your boyfriend.' The words were out before Jo could stop herself. She didn't normally interfere in her daughter's relationships, but she liked Ben and she definitely had reservations about Jack.

'Oh, Mum. Ben's OK, but ... ' Her face flushed and Joanne forced a smile.

'I know,' she said. 'He's a bit young. But Jack?'

'Don't say anything, Mum,' Lucy interrupted. 'I know you don't like him.'

Jo thought it wouldn't do any good to keep on about it so she changed the subject, saying, 'I've got something interesting to show you after dinner.'

When they'd eaten, she was about to get the picture out of her bag when her phone rang.

'It's Auntie Liz,' she said, carrying the phone and sitting back down at the table.

'Is she OK?' Lucy asked.

Jo flapped her hand. 'Wait a minute,' she said, pressing the phone to her ear. 'Liz, Liz, slow down. It's OK. We can cope.'

She nodded as her sister continued.

'I'm not prepared,' Liz wailed. 'I thought I had plenty of time to make arrangements.'

'Don't worry. It's not a problem,' Jo interrupted. 'I'll come over first thing in the morning. I'll phone Clive straight away. I'm sure he'll understand.'

'But you've only just started the job and you've got the builders in. I'm so sorry to be such a nuisance,' Liz said.

She was near to tears and Jo tried to reassure her.

'We knew you were going into hospital some time. It's a good thing they've brought it forward. Better to get it over with.'

When Liz finally ran out of steam, Jo put the phone down with a sigh.

'What was that all about?' Lucy asked.

'They've had a cancellation. They want her to go in tomorrow.'

'And the cousins are coming to stay

here?' Lucy pulled a face. 'I thought you were going to move into Auntie Liz's while she was in hospital.'

'That was the plan. But I can't move out of here and leave the workmen to get on with it. If the kids stay here I can drop them off at school in the mornings and then go on to work, as well as keep an eye on what's happening here.'

Lucy pouted. 'I'll still be here, and Auntie Liz will be home before I leave for uni. I could keep you up to date on how the work's going.'

'I'm sure you could. But I think this is a better arrangement.'

'You don't trust me,' Lucy said.

'Of course I do. Don't be silly. It's just … you know how I worry.' Jo attempted a little laugh, but it was true in part. It wasn't that she didn't trust her daughter — it was the thought of Jack Wilson hanging around that disturbed her. 'Anyway, I'd better phone Clive and tell him I'll be late tomorrow.'

She had already told him that her sister was due to go into hospital and that she would be looking after her nephew and two nieces. He'd been very understanding about her possible need to have time off, but she was a bit worried about the short notice. Liz had originally been given a date two months ahead; plenty of time to make arrangements, they'd thought.

To her relief, Clive told her to take all the time she needed. When she put the phone down Lucy was still frowning.

'I won't have to give up my room, will I?' she asked.

'Of course not. We'll sort something out.' While she had been talking to Liz, Jo's mind had been busy mulling over the options. The house had three bedrooms and a box room, but a lot of stuff was still piled up in the smaller room waiting for the renovations to be finished before unpacking. There was space for a camp bed, though, which would do for Edward. The two girls could share the spare room. She smiled to herself. A good job they'd had the bathroom and en suite fitted before starting on the kitchen, she thought. And with a bit of luck the shower would be finished tomorrow.

She was up very early the next morning and started organising the spare room while she was still in her dressing gown. Lucy hadn't got up by the time she had made up the beds and had a slurp of coffee.

'No time for breakfast,' she muttered, glancing at her watch and going to the foot of the stairs. 'About time you got up, Lucy,' she called.

She had to get over to Liz's house on the other side of town, take her to the hospital and then drop the children off at school. There was no reason for Lucy to get up really, but Jo didn't like the thought of her lounging around in bed. Hadn't she said she was going to do some research at the library? She looked at her watch again, tempted to go up and rouse her. But it was getting late so she shrugged and picked up her bag.

As she was about to leave, the back door opened. She gasped as Lucy came in, still in her dressing gown. Her hair was tangled and her slippers were caked with mud. She rubbed her eyes and murmured, 'Morning, Mum. You off then?'

'Lucy, what were you doing outside in your night things?'

'Couldn't sleep. I thought I heard someone outside so I went down to investigate.'

'You should have called me. Suppose it had been a burglar?' The suspicion that she might have been meeting Jack crossed her mind but she kept quiet. Surely he wouldn't have been hanging around at this time of the morning?

'Don't be daft, Mum. As if I'd tackle a burglar.' Lucy laughed, but the laugh turned to a puzzled frown. 'I thought I heard a child crying. Must have been dreaming.' She rubbed her eyes again and shivered.

'You're freezing,' Jo said, massaging Lucy's hands. 'Go and get dressed. And put everything in the washing machine, your slippers too.'

'OK. Have a good day, Mum.' Lucy paused with her hand on the banister. 'I just remembered — you're picking up the cousins aren't you? I'll cook something nice for their tea.'

Jo kissed her daughter's cheek. 'Thanks, love. Now, I must be off.'

As she started the car she reflected that Lucy was a good girl, despite the occasional strops. Perhaps she should rely on her daughter's good sense and stop worrying about Jack Wilson. But she couldn't help feeling relieved that Jack would be working at Grayling Manor today instead of at the New Rectory. What worried her more than anything, though, was that it wasn't the first time Lucy had gone out into the garden in her night things. What was going on? Could she really be sleep-walking? She had seemed very confused when she came indoors.

Jo was tempted to confide in Liz, but when she arrived at her sister's house, Liz was in the hall, her holdall at her feet. She looked up with relief as Jo came in, holding up her mobile.

'I was just about to call you.'

'Sorry. I'm here now.' How could she pile more worry on Liz, who was already anxious about the coming operation? 'Where are the kids?' she asked, pushing her own concerns to the back of her mind.

'In the kitchen. They're all ready. I don't have much time to get to the hospital so can you drop me off there then take the kids to school?' She raised her voice. 'Edward, Rosie, Amy — come along. Auntie Jo's here.'

The girls rushed into the hall, throwing their arms round Joanne's legs.

'Are we going to stay at your house?' Rosie asked.

'Just for a few days, till Mummy's better,' Jo said.

'I like your house,' Amy said. 'When we came last time that man said he'd put a swing in the garden for us.'

Jo raised her eyebrows and looked at Liz over the little girl's head.

'What man?' mouthed Liz.

Jo shrugged. Must be blooming Jack again, she thought. He seemed to be worming his way into her family. She thrust the thought away. 'Come on, then. We'd better get a move on. Where's Edward?'

Rosie frowned. 'He's being a pain. Said he wants to stay here.'

'Well, he can't,' Liz snapped, striding into the kitchen. 'Come on, Edward. We haven't got all day.'

Edward was still sitting in the kitchen, kicking his feet against the table leg.

'I don't want to stay at Auntie Jo's,' he mumbled.

'We've talked about this. Now stop being so silly.'

He slid off the chair and mooched towards the door.

In the car the children were rather subdued and there were tearful goodbyes at the hospital.

'I don't want you to go in there, Mummy,' Rosie wailed.

Jo did her best to reassure them, but when they arrived at the school, they were reluctant to get out of the car as it dawned on them that their aunt would be picking them up from school instead of their mother.

'It's only for a few days, and when Mummy comes home she'll be all better,' she said.

'Will she be able to take us swimming like she used to?' Amy asked.

'Of course. And she said when Daddy comes home you're all going on a nice holiday.'

This seemed to cheer the girls up but Edward still looked unhappy. Jo saw with relief that the other children were going inside and she urged her nieces and nephew to follow them. The head teacher was standing in the doorway and she went over to explain why she would be picking the children up later.

The school had already been informed that Liz would be going into hospital soon and she had phoned them as soon as she'd got the message yesterday.

'Don't worry, Mrs Mason. We'll keep an eye on them. It's very stressful for little ones when something like this happens,' the teacher said.

145

'The girls seem fine but I'm worried about Edward,' Jo said.

'We'll look after him and phone you if there's a problem.' The woman smiled reassuringly, but as Jo went back to her car she was still worried. She sighed. Coping with a new house and job was stressful enough, but three small children … Had she taken on too much? But she couldn't let Liz down.

10

When Jo arrived at the Manor she forced herself to concentrate on sorting through the old manuscripts. Getting immersed in work helped to take her mind off the worry about Liz and, to a lesser extent, Edward. She was sure that once the operation was over and he knew when his mother was coming home he would cheer up. It wasn't like him to sulk and act up. Usually he was a sunny-natured child. But having your mother go into hospital was worrying for anyone, let alone for an eight-year-old.

Halfway through the morning, Clive came in to check on her progress and she showed him the rest of photographs from the previous day.

'I'm not sure if we can do anything with these,' she said, handing him a batch of water-damaged prints.

'It would be a shame to lose them,'

he said. 'They are part of the house's history. Leave them with me and I'll try to find a restorer. They can do wonders on computers these days.'

As she put the pictures in an envelope she remembered the photo she'd taken home. She hadn't had a chance to show it to Lucy, and in the hurry to get Liz to the hospital and the children to school this morning she had forgotten all about it.

She fished it out of her bag. 'I hope you don't mind, Clive. I took this one home to show my daughter. It was in the box with the others. I thought it could be the house that was there before mine was built.'

He took it from her and held it up to the light.

'Looks like it. It says St Mark's Rectory. I wonder what it was doing here?'

'Did your family have any connection with the people who lived there?' Jo asked.

'I haven't come across anything so far.'

'Neither have I — but then, I wouldn't know the name of whoever lived there that long ago anyway.'

Clive frowned. 'It's a bit of a coincidence, isn't it, you being the one to find it.'

She peered at the picture again, remembering the foundations that Lucy and Jack had uncovered.

'One of the workmen uncovered something that looks like the foundations of a much bigger house,' she said. 'The original building must have covered twice as much ground.'

'It's probably nothing to do with the Graylings. The photo could have been left here by anyone, I suppose.'

When he'd gone back to work, Jo switched on the scanner, a little disappointed that he hadn't shown more interest. She'd been hoping he could help solve the mystery. But then, they were researching the history of Grayling Manor and Clive's family, not her new home.

She managed to get quite a lot of work done, and by lunchtime it was a relief to go outside for some air. She walked a little way down the drive and got out her mobile to phone the hospital.

Liz was out of surgery and in the recovery ward.

'Everything went very well. She should be home in a few days,' the nurse said. 'You can visit this evening.'

Jo thanked her and let out a breath. She hadn't realised how worried she'd been. She would take the children with her tonight to visit. When Edward saw that his mother was all right, he might settle down a bit, she thought. It was a pity Mike was away on business just now. The kids needed their father at a time like this. Still, it had always been a distinct possibility that he wouldn't be around at whatever point Liz had her operation. They were probably used to his frequent absences, and in the normal run of things, Liz coped very well on her own.

It was much cooler now that autumn was here and Jo was determined to make the most of any remaining fine weather. She found a seat out of the wind and sat down to eat her sandwiches, turning her face up to the sun. She used to love this time of year, but the anniversary of Tom's death was approaching and she knew the next couple of weeks would be hard. Thank goodness she had the children to look after, she thought. There would be no time to brood with three little ones running about the house.

Clive had given her permission to leave early to pick up the children from school so she cut her lunch break short. Back at her desk, she found herself constantly being drawn to the portrait of the solemn-looking young woman called Sophie. She looked sad in this picture, a complete contrast to the group photo with her family around her.

Shrugging, she placed the picture in the scanner and saved it to the file she was building. On impulse she printed off a copy of both Sophie's photo, and the photo of St Mark's Rectory, and put them in her bag. She'd show both to Lucy when she got home. The name Blandford seemed vaguely familiar and she scrolled back through the names she'd added to the family tree. But she couldn't find anything, and anyway, she didn't have time to ponder the mystery as the children would be coming out of school soon. Clive was busy in another part of the house so she left a post-it note on her computer screen explaining how far she'd got with today's research.

Since moving into the New Rectory and cycling everywhere, she had almost forgotten what it was like to fight the traffic jams to get into town. As she neared the school she found cars parked all along the road and had to go round the corner before she could find a space. She got out and hurried back to the entrance just as her nieces came out, laughing and chattering to their friends. At least they didn't seem too upset about their mother's hospitalisation. But where was Edward?

'Where is your brother?' she asked Rose.

'He had to stay behind,' the little girl said.

'What's he been up to?'

'Don't know.'

'Wait in the car with Amy. I'll have to go and fetch him.'

Jo hurried off, fighting to hold back her frustration. It was so unlike Edward to play up like this.

She reached the entrance just as Edward's teacher came out, holding him by the hand.

'Oh, there you are, Mrs Mason,' she said. 'I'm sorry about this. I've had to give Edward a good talking to.'

'Why? What's he done?'

'He pulled Sarah's hair and made her cry.'

'Oh, Edward, that wasn't very nice.' Jo bent down and looked into the little boy's eyes. 'What made you do a thing like that?'

'When I told her my mum was in hospital, she said she was going to die.' He looked up at her, tears almost brimming over. 'She's not, is she?'

Jo put her arms around him and hugged him.

'Of course not. Sarah's a very silly girl to say something like that.' She looked

153

over his head at the teacher. 'I thought you were going to keep an eye on him, make sure he got through the day all right. I told the head about his mum being in hospital.'

'I'm sorry, Mrs Mason. I try to be fair, but Edward wouldn't tell me what Sarah said.'

Jo was still angry, but with the teacher now, not Edward. She led him away, still with her arm around him.

'Let's go and find the girls,' she said. 'Then we'll go to the hospital. Mum's had her operation and everything's fine. They said you can go in and see her, so you'll be able to see for yourself that she's OK.'

Edward managed a smile but he still looked a bit upset.

'Don't worry, we won't tell Mum about this,' Jo said.

⋆   ⋆   ⋆

Liz was sitting up in bed when they arrived. She looked rather pale but her eyes brightened when the children came in. She hugged each in turn but she winced when Edward clung to her. He wouldn't let go so Jo gently eased him away and asked him to fetch a chair for her.

When he came back, she sat down and took her sister's hand.

'You OK?' she asked.

'Just glad it's all over,' Liz said.

'When are you coming home, Mummy?' Rosie asked.

'I'm not sure. I'll have to wait and see what the doctor says.'

'How long will we have to stay at Auntie Jo's then?' Edward asked.

'It won't be for long,' she assured him.

Edward frowned and looked at the floor, kicking against the chair leg. Jo shook her head and pulled a face.

'I don't know what's got into him. He used to like coming to stay with me,' she whispered, patting Liz's hand. 'Don't worry. He'll be OK.'

'I can't thank you enough for looking after them,' Liz said.

'It's my pleasure. I love having them,' Jo said. It was true. In the past she'd always welcomed any opportunity to spend time with Liz's children. But this was under different, more stressful circumstances, so no wonder Edward was finding it hard. And if Jo was honest, she was finding it hard too. It wasn't only the concern over her sister's health; there was the stress of settling into her new job, as well as the ongoing work on the house. At least the children would be at school most of the time, she thought, smiling at Liz. 'I'll cope. You just concentrate on getting well and let me worry about the kids.'

She could see Liz was getting tired so she stood up.

'Time to go, let Mummy get some rest.'

They didn't want to leave, but fortunately a nurse came in and drew the curtains round Liz's bed.

'Time for Mummy's medicine,' she said brightly. 'You can come back and see her tomorrow.'

Liz kissed them all in turn and waved forlornly as they reluctantly moved away.

'See you tomorrow, Sis,' Jo said. 'Take care.'

Amy was struggling not to cry and Edward looked on the verge of tears too. Jo sighed and took a deep breath.

'Come on kids, cheer up. Mum will be home soon. I know, let's go to McDonald's.'

'Mum doesn't let us. Only when we're on holiday,' Rosie said.

'Well, let's pretend we're on holiday,' Jo said. Anything to take their minds off their mother lying pale and listless in her hospital bed. She had planned a healthy meal, determined to live up to her sister's principles, especially as she and Lucy had been living on takeaways while the kitchen was being refurbished. Still, it wouldn't hurt for once, she decided.

At the restaurant she got out her mobile and rang Lucy to tell her where they were. After reassuring her that her aunt was recovering well, she said, 'You can cook yourself something, can't you, love? Or come and join us here.'

'We've already eaten,' Lucy said.

'We?' Jo groaned inwardly. Not Jack again.

'Ben was here. You don't mind, do you? He's helping me with my research.'

'No, of course not. How's it coming on?'

'We found a book in the library with pictures of old houses. And Jack's uncovered some more foundation stones. It's definitely the remains of the old house,' Lucy said.

So Jack was at the house too. Jo hoped the excitement in her daughter's voice was caused by enthusiasm for their discovery and not by the presence of the good-looking but far too worldly-wise kitchen fitter.

'The kids are enjoying their burgers but we've nearly finished so we'll be home soon. You can tell me all about it then,' she said, before saying her goodbyes and turning her attention to the children. They were eating hungrily and she was pleased that the worry over their mother didn't seem to have spoiled their appetites. Even Edward had polished off the lot.

On the way home he began to tease his sisters and Jo's heart lifted when she heard them giggling in the back of the car.

But on the approach to the New Rectory they became subdued, as the realisation sank in that they were not going home.

She pulled up in the drive and got out.

'Out you get, kids. It's getting late.'

Amy ran up to the front door. 'I wonder if that man's been and put up our swing,' she said.

'I don't like him,' Edward said, the surly tone back. 'Or those other children.'

Jo hoped Jack had already left. Edward was quite capable of being rude in this mood and she couldn't cope with it.

'I expect he's been too busy,' she said. 'Besides, it's too late to play in the garden now.'

She ushered the children into the kitchen where she was relieved to see Lucy and Ben sitting close together at the table, their heads bent over a large book — and no Jack.

'Hi, Mum. Auntie Liz OK?' Lucy asked.

'She's fine. Should be home in a few days.' Jo went over to the sink to fill the kettle. 'Who's for hot chocolate?' she asked, pausing as she caught sight of movement outside the window.

'I thought Jack had gone home,' she said.

Lucy came over and peered through the window.

'Mum, there's nobody there.' She lowered the blind and switched on the light. 'Go and sit down. I'll make the drinks.'

Jo lifted a corner of the blind and looked again, but she couldn't see anyone. I'm tired, just imagining things, she told herself. But the suspicion lingered that it had been Jack out there. Why was he lurking around? Was he really interested in Lucy, or was there another reason for his interest in the house? Thank goodness she didn't have any valuables worth selling. Not that she really thought he would burgle the place. She still felt uneasy though and she shivered a little as Lucy placed the mug of hot chocolate in front of her.

'There, this'll warm you up, Mum,' she said. 'Do you think we should put the heating on? It has turned a bit chilly.'

'It's a bit early for that,' Jo said, thinking of her finances. 'I'm fine, really. Just a bit tired, that's all.' She turned to the children who were enjoying their chocolate. 'Drink up. It's bed time.'

The girls went up quite happily and Jo smiled as she listened to them splashing in the bath. But she was still worried about Edward who was sitting on the bottom stair, his lips tight, his arms folded across his chest.

'What are you hanging about there for?' Jo asked.

'I don't want to sleep here. I want to go home,' he said.

'Don't be silly, Edward. You can't stay at home on your own.'

'I can. I'm big enough to look after myself. Mum says I'm very grown up for my age.'

Jo knew that Liz often told the little

161

boy that he was the man of the house while his father was away. It helped him to cope with Mike's frequent absences.

She crouched down beside him.

'Your mum's right,' she said. 'Which is why I need your help. I'm relying on you to help with the girls, as I'm sure you do when you're at home with Mum. Besides, you don't want her worrying about you, do you?'

Edward shook his head.

'Right then. Up you go.' Jo stood up and took his hand. He reluctantly followed her, hesitating at the door of the little box room where he was to sleep.

The girls were out of the bath and romping on the beds in their room. She gave Edward a gentle push in the direction of the bathroom and left him to it.

When Amy and Rosie were settled she went to find Edward, only to realise that he was still playing around in the bathroom instead of in his bed. Determined to stay calm, she persuaded him to get into bed and went to turn the light out.

'Can you leave it on please, Auntie?' he said.

'Oh, Edward, you're a big boy now,' Jo protested. But seeing the misery on the child's face she relented. After all, it was his first night in a strange house. 'I'll leave the door open and the landing light on. Is that OK?'

He nodded and she bent and kissed his cheek before saying goodnight and hurrying out of the room.

Downstairs, Lucy wanted to show her the book with the pictures of the Rectory but Jo struggled to summon up any real interest. Although she enjoyed it, it was always exhausting looking after the three young children.

At ten o'clock she stood up and rubbed her eyes. 'Sorry, I'm shattered. I must go to bed, love. Let's talk about it tomorrow.'

She was so tired she fell asleep almost as soon as she got into bed but it seemed only a moment before she jerked awake. What was that noise? Heart thumping, she sat up, ears straining. A child was crying. She was about to get up and investigate which of the children it was when the door opened and Edward came in.

'Can I get in with you, Auntie Jo? I can't sleep and I'm so cold.'

Jo took hold of him by the shoulders, peering into his face by the light from the landing but there was no sign of tears. It must have been one of the girls.

'You really ought to go back to bed, Edward,' she said, taking his hand and leading him back to his room. But as she went in she shivered. It *was* cold — freezing in fact. She couldn't expect the little boy to sleep in here. She took him back to her room and tucked him in.

'I'm just going to check on the girls,' she said. 'Go to sleep.'

First thing tomorrow she would have to phone the heating engineers. Again. They obviously hadn't connected everything up properly. More hassle she thought, turning over and pulling the duvet up over her shoulder.

11

1890

It had been raining for days and the children were restless from being cooped up indoors for so long. Edward had been particularly naughty, teasing his sisters mercilessly and drawing disapproving sighs from his mother.

Thomas's solution to the children's naughtiness was to set them more lessons, or make them learn Bible verses off by heart but Sophie tried to make things easier for them, feeling that their father was sometimes a little too strict. She was getting bored herself, longing to get out in the garden among her flowers. Autumn was fast turning to winter and there would not be many more opportunities for her and the children to get out of the house. She dreaded the long, dark days with only Thomas for company and parish duties to keep her occupied.

This morning however, nothing would jolt Edward out of his bad mood. While Amelia and Rosalind sat at the table colouring in the pictures in their storybook, he stood by the window, staring moodily out at the rain and kicking against the wall.

'Don't do that, Edward,' Sophie said. 'Why don't you come and do some drawing?'

'Don't want to,' the boy said, giving an extra hard kick. 'I want to go down to the stable and see Chummy. He hasn't been out for days.'

'Bill has been exercising him. Now, Edward, please do as you're told and come away from the window.'

If only Margaret were here to take them off her hands, Sophie thought. But she had given the girl leave to visit her sick mother again, and take her a few things from the Rectory pantry. Thomas would disapprove, saying it was bad form to mollycoddle the servants, she thought with a sigh. But she knew the

Chapman family were poor and she was glad to be able to help out. For, despite her disapproval of Margaret's behaviour with Philip, she could not fault the girl's work. She was a good nursemaid and patience itself with the children, especially Edward, always able to cajole him into apologising to the girls and find things to occupy his restless spirit.

Edward was still sulking and Sophie glanced at him in irritation. If he carried on like this she would have to threaten him with a visit to his father's study. She hated being heavy-handed with the children, always trying to maintain a balance between kindness and discipline, but it was hard sometimes.

Forcing herself to smile she examined the girls' crayoning with interest, then turned to Edward.

'Why don't you finish your model train?'

'I did that ages ago. I want to go out.'

'But it's pouring with rain.'

'Don't care.'

Sophie glanced up with relief as the door opened.

'Here's Margaret back from visiting her mother.' She turned to the maid. 'How is she?'

'A little better, Ma'am. She thanks you for the things you sent.' Margaret seemed a little breathless, as if she had been running, and Sophie looked at her in concern.

'Are you all right? You did not have to hurry back. I can quite easily see to the children's lunch.'

'I ran, Ma'am.' She took a deep breath. 'I took a short cut through the woods and thought someone was following me.'

'But who?'

'I think it was that Joe. The black-smith's apprentice. He wants me to walk out with him.'

'Would that be such a bad thing, Margaret?' Sophie thought young Joe would be a far more suitable match for the nursemaid and would perhaps make her see that a liaison with Philip could not ever work. But Margaret's next words caused her heart to sink.

'I don't like him, Ma'am. He keeps

pestering me.'

'If you want him to stop bothering you, I could ask my husband to have a word with him.'

'Oh, no, Ma'am, don't do that.' Margaret's face blanched. 'I don't want to cause any trouble.'

'Very well, we'll leave it for now. But you must let me know if he's being a nuisance.' Sophie sighed inwardly. A man with a good steady trade, as Joe would be when he finished his apprenticeship, would make a good husband. If only she was attracted to him rather than Philip, a son of the lord of the Manor. But Sophie well knew that you did not choose who you fell in love with. Sometimes it just happened with all the suddenness and randomness of a lightning bolt.

They had been speaking in low voices but were interrupted when Edward asked, 'When's Uncle Philip coming back?'

Sophie smiled, glad to change the subject, although she could have wished that he had not mentioned his uncle at that moment.

'Any day now. He may even have arrived already. I'm sure he'll find time to visit us while he's home.'

Amelia jumped down from the table and ran to her mother. 'Goody. I like it when he comes to see us. He makes everything fun.'

'Well, it'll probably only be a short visit. He'll want to spend time with Alice while he's home,' Sophie said with a covert glance at Margaret. She had hoped that an absence of a few weeks would have been sufficient to cool the maid's feelings towards her brother. But she could tell from the stricken look on the girl's face that mention of Philip's fiancée had upset her.

Perhaps it would be better if she dissuaded Philip from visiting this time. After all, he was only home for a few days. And if the children wanted to spend time with their uncle, she could take them up to the Manor. They had not seen their grandparents for some time anyway.

★ ★ ★

The following day it was still raining and the children were more fractious than ever. They were used to spending time outdoors after their morning lessons, either playing on the swing that Philip had erected, or riding their pony in the field behind the Rectory.

Sophie's patience was wearing thin and she was relieved when lesson time ended and Margaret came to take the children upstairs to wash and get ready for luncheon.

Thomas had been out all morning visiting his parishioners. He would not let the heavy downpour stop him from going about his duties. However, he was not in a very good mood when he joined the family at the dining table. The children, sensing this, were subdued, and ate their meal in silence.

As they were finishing, there was a knock at the front door and Thomas pushed his chair back, anticipating a request to call on a sick villager. But when Ruby came in it was to announce that a groom from the Manor had ridden over with a message.

She handed the note to Sophie and said, 'He's waiting for an answer, Ma'am.'

'It's from Father,' Sophie said, tearing it open. 'Philip's home. We're invited for dinner tonight, all of us.'

'All of us? Do you mean the children too?' Thomas asked.

Sophie nodded.

'But it's far too late for them to stay up. And they're too young to eat with the family.'

'Father says we can stay at the Manor overnight. The children can sleep in the nursery. They see far too little of the family in spite of us living so near.'

'Very well, my dear. But we must return home first thing in the morning. I must not neglect my parishioners.'

'Thank you, Thomas.' Sophie got up and dropped a kiss on his head. 'I know you find these family gatherings tedious but I do like to spend time with my parents. They are not getting any younger, you know. And they do enjoy seeing the children.'

'Very well. Now, you must let me get on with my work. Perhaps I can finish sorting out the parish records before it is time for us to leave for the Manor.'

'Yes, dear,' Sophie said meekly.

Fortunately, it had stopped raining and she sent the children out in the garden to play so that they would not disturb their father. He was quite capable of forbidding them from visiting their grandparents if they displeased him.

She rang for Ruby to clear the table. 'And when that's done, run down to the stable and tell Bill we shall need the pony and trap later,' she said.

She went upstairs to the nursery, where Margaret was sitting by the fire doing some mending. When she told the nurse-maid about the invitation to the Manor, the girl looked up and said, 'Will you need me, Ma'am?'

'Yes. We are going to stay overnight so you will have to see to the children.'

'I'll pack a bag then, Ma'am, shall I?' Margaret's voice did not betray any excitement at the prospect of visiting

Grayling Manor and Sophie wondered if she knew Philip was home. Perhaps she ought to mention it in order to gauge the girl's reaction to mention of his name.

Taking a deep breath she said, 'My brother is home for the half term break. The children are looking forward to seeing him.'

As she had feared, Margaret flushed scarlet and turned away quickly to fetch the children's night clothes from the chest of drawers. So she was still enamoured of him then, Sophie thought. Too late to nip it in the bud now. She should have realised how serious things were months ago. She could only hope that for Philip it had been a mere summer dalliance.

Resolving not to speak to Margaret about it until she had seen her brother, she took the clothing the maid had sorted and packed it into the small overnight bag.

'I'll finish this,' she said. 'Go and see what the children are doing. They should come indoors now. And keep them quiet. The master is working in his study.'

'Yes, Ma'am.' She bobbed a curtsey

and left the room.

Sophie wandered over to the window and looked down the garden, smiling as Edward pushed Rosalind on the swing. They had enjoyed playing on it so much and she blessed Philip for his thoughtfulness. Soon the weather would change and the children would be cooped up indoors. Sophie dreaded the winter and the impossibility of keeping them entertained so that they did not disturb their father too much. It was such a strain anticipating her husband's moods but she felt guilty for being so relieved whenever parish business took him out of the house.

The children burst into the room dispelling her sombre mood and she smiled. She must count her blessings, she told herself, looking down at their rosy faces, sharing their excitement at the prospect of spending an evening with their grandparents and the rest of the family.

Alice would be there too and surely, seeing her and Philip together, Margaret must realise how hopeless any dream of a lasting relationship with him was.

* * *

Sophie looked around the vast dining table, smiling at the rare sight of her family gathered all together. Flowers from the hothouse decorated the table and the silverware gleamed in the light of the candelabra. Portraits of Grayling forebears looked down on them from the walls and a cheerful log fire burned in the huge stone fireplace.

To her relief, the children were on their best behaviour, enjoying the treat of being allowed to dine with the grown-ups. Thomas would have no cause for complaint today.

Her smile faded however, when her eyes rested on her older brother. Robert looked tired and drawn, and although he professed himself fully recovered from the illness that had debilitated him during the summer months, Sophie wasn't convinced.

Perhaps taking over the running of the estate was proving too much for him in his weakened condition. She was sure

Father could do more but he seemed bent on enjoying the privileges of the landed gentry without putting in the hard work necessary to keep things going.

And then there was Philip. Another worry. Sophie sighed, although she could not fault his behaviour this evening. Alice sat at his right-hand side and he seemed most attentive, bending his head to listen to whatever she was saying.

She turned to her father.

'It's so nice to have us all together, Father, isn't it. I expect you'll miss Philip when he goes back to Oxford.'

Before her father could reply Philip looked up and said, 'I may not go back.'

'What?' Thomas spluttered into his soup. Without bothering to wipe his mouth with his napkin he continued, 'But you must. You only have a couple more terms before you sit for your degree and then you will be ready to take up your commission.'

'But I'm not going to join the army, brother-in-law.'

Thomas spluttered again, his face

reddening. 'Not ... ?'

Robert intervened. 'It has already been discussed. That is why Philip has come home — to make arrangements.'

'But I thought it was all settled,' Thomas said.

Philip pushed his chair back and stood up. 'It is nothing to do with you.'

Alice laid a gentle hand on his arm but he shook her off.

Sophie thought he was about to storm out of the room but he ran his hand through his hair and sighed, sitting down once more and picking up his soup spoon.

After an embarrassed silence, everyone resumed their meal. The children were wide-eyed, never having seen their uncle lose his temper before. But they were used to their father's moods and took refuge in being quiet and finishing their soup.

Amelia looked very upset though, and when the soup course was finished and the maids came to clear, Sophie asked one of them to fetch Margaret to take the little girls up to bed.

'I can stay up though, can't I, Mama,' Edward said.

'Of course you may,' Sophie said, after a quick glance at Thomas.

When Margaret came to fetch the children she kept her eyes downcast, avoiding looking at Philip. Sophie hoped she was the only one present who noticed her brother's yearning look in the nursemaid's direction. But emotions were still running high after his outburst. Any tension in the atmosphere would probably be put down to this.

She spoke quietly to Margaret, saying that the girls could have their dessert in the nursery.

'Very well, Ma'am,' said Margaret, ushering them out of the room.

After the children had left, the main course was brought in and the conversation resumed.

Thomas turned to Sophie.

'You haven't mentioned this before. Why not?'

'Nothing had been decided until now.

Besides, I knew you would be disappointed after your efforts on Philip's behalf.'

'So, Philip, what are you going to do with your life then, in the absence of a good career?' Thomas asked.

'As you know, Robert has not been at all well. He has been finding the running of the estate too much for him, so I am going to take over.'

'Sir, are you agreeable to this?' Thomas addressed his father-in-law, who so far had not said anything, appearing to be more interested in his roast beef and the glass of wine at his elbow.

James Grayling looked up now and said, 'It seems a sensible solution.'

Robert started coughing and they waited until he had regained his breath.

'It is only a temporary measure, until I am fit again.'

'Which I am sure won't be long,' Sophie said with an affectionate glance at him.

Robert took his wife's hand. 'We are going abroad for the winter, to the south of France.'

'Plenty of sunshine is what the doctor ordered,' Jane said. 'It will be good for Robert to get away from the dreary English winter for a few months. When we return, Philip will be free to take up any career he desires.'

'It makes sense I suppose,' Thomas muttered. 'But Philip, you have been enjoying your time at Oxford, although perhaps not devoting as much time to your studies as you should. Running the estate will not be much fun for you.'

Philip gave a short laugh. 'I don't suppose the army would be much fun either. Don't worry, dear brother-in-law, I will do my duty.'

Sophie bit her lip. She hated it when members of her family did not agree, but Thomas had always been prone to thinking he knew best for everybody and was not averse to voicing his opinions whether it upset people or not. What difference did it make to him what Philip chose to do? But in this instance, she almost had to agree with her husband. Philip's continued presence at home could only spell disaster if he persisted in his infatuation with Margaret. They would not be able to keep their feelings secret for much longer and Sophie dreaded the consequences when the rest of the family realised what was going on.

The tension in the room eased somewhat as Alice spoke up. She was usually so quiet that those round the table looked round in surprise as she leaned across and took her fiancé's hand.

'Well I, for one, am delighted that Philip will be spending more time at home.' She turned a beaming smile on him. 'I have missed you so much,' she said.

Philip flushed in embarrassment but he smiled and said, 'I've missed you too, my dear. But I'm afraid we won't be able to spend much time together. I shall be kept extremely busy on the estate.'

'It will be different when you are married and you take your place here,' said James. 'With Jane and Robert away, you will be the mistress of Grayling Manor.'

Sophie sensed that Philip was

beginning to feel a little uncomfortable with being the centre of attention. He clearly did not want to talk about his forthcoming marriage.

To change the subject she asked her father if he would like more wine, gesturing to the butler to bring another bottle. 'And I think we're ready for dessert,' she said.

When the food was served she asked Robert where they would be staying in France and for the rest of the evening the conversation stayed amicable. There was no further reference to Philip's future, although Thomas was very quiet and Sophie could sense his disapproval.

As they finished their meal, Robert endured another bout of coughing and he and Jane excused themselves and went to their room. Their departure brought the long evening to a close and Alice's father sent for the carriage to take them home. But when she and her parents said their goodnights there was no sign of Philip.

'Where is the boy?' James Grayling muttered. 'Never here when he's wanted.'

'Never mind,' said Alice. 'He said something about speaking to the groom about his horse. We are going riding tomorrow so I'll see him then.'

Thomas and James repaired to the library for a nightcap and Sophie took Edward up to the nursery.

The girls were asleep but Margaret wasn't there. Perhaps she had gone down to the kitchen for a drink. But Sophie had a feeling that she had slipped out to the stables to meet Philip.

'Edward, don't forget to clean your teeth. I'll be back in a minute,' she said.

She hurried down the back stairs, hoping that she would encounter the nursemaid on her way up. But there was no sign of her and she opened the back door, glancing across the yard. Goodness knows what they were up to. She must catch them and break it up before her brother did something he would later regret.

A sliver of moon peeked through the clouds, reflecting off the still-damp cobbles and Sophie was able to see her way across the stable yard. As she approached the tack room, one of the horses stamped its hooves and blew out a snorting breath, making her jump. She stood still for a moment, listening. Quiet voices broke the silence of the night and she strained to hear, breathing a sigh of relief. If they were talking they could not be doing anything they shouldn't.

She was about to confront the couple when Philip's voice rose. 'I am not going to marry her, I promise. It's you I love.'

'But your family ... ' Margaret's voice held a hint of despair.

'They can't make me. It might be different if I were the eldest son.'

'But, Philip, what are we going to do?'

'Don't worry, my love. It will be all right.'

Embarrassed at eavesdropping, Sophie moved nearer and peered around the open door, intending to make her presence known. Philip was holding Margaret in his arms, stroking her hair and trying to comfort her, and Sophie drew back. How could she interrupt this tender scene, a reminder of her own lost love so many years ago?

She stumbled a little as she retreated and Philip looked round, alerted by the slight noise. He hastily let Margaret go, turning to face his sister.

'What are you doing out here at this time of night?' he asked.

'I could ask you that,' Sophie retorted. She turned to Margaret. 'Go back to the house at once. The children need you,' she said.

'Ma'am, please — I'm sorry. I didn't mean ... ' She choked back a sob, pushed past her employer and ran across the yard.

'Margaret, wait.' Philip took a few steps after her but the girl was gone. He turned to his sister.

'Sophie, it's not her fault,' he said. 'I asked her to meet me here. I had to see her.' His face was contorted with pain. 'You don't understand.'

'Of course I do, Philip. But you must see ... ' Sophie laid a hand on his arm. 'It has to stop before you do something

186

you regret. So far you've been lucky. I don't think anyone suspects, but if Father should get to hear ... '

'I — we — haven't done anything wrong,' the young man protested. 'I would never do anything to hurt Margaret.'

'And what about Alice? She would be terribly hurt if she knew.'

'Her pride would be hurt. She doesn't care about me. This betrothal was arranged by our families — we had little say in the matter.'

'Nevertheless, you have made a commitment to her.'

Philip covered his face with his hands and groaned. 'Sophie, what am I going to do?'

She took his arm and urged him out of the stable and across the yard.

'You know what you must do,' she said. 'Your duty. Now come on in. It's late and we all need our sleep.'

She opened the door quietly and they crept up the back stairs to their rooms. A lamp burned on the main landing but it was very quiet and Sophie hoped that everyone had gone to bed. She whispered a goodnight to Philip and opened the door to her room.

Thomas was seated at a small table by the window writing and he looked up as she came in.

'I thought you had gone to bed. Where were you?'

'Seeing to the children,' she lied, hoping he would not notice the flush that rose to her cheeks.

'We have a nursemaid for that,' he replied, standing up and taking off his dressing gown. 'I thought maybe you were trying to talk some sense into that brother of yours. His behaviour at dinner was appalling.'

'I agree, Thomas, but he's young and impulsive.'

'Time he grew up then.'

Sophie did not want to get into yet another argument about her brother and went into the adjoining dressing room without replying. When she came back Thomas was already in bed and, as she

188

climbed in beside him, she hoped he would not start again. To her relief he just leaned over and turned out the lamp without a word.

She lay down and tried to sleep. But she could not dispel the feeling of apprehension left by her conversation with Philip. This whole mess was sure to end badly, whatever course of action her brother took.

★   ★   ★

Sophie woke with a headache after a restless night. She could not dispel the feeling of doom which engulfed her whenever she thought about her brother and the nursemaid. What was she going to do about it? If Thomas discovered what was going on, he would force her to dismiss Margaret at once. He would not tolerate the slightest hint of impropriety. But Margaret would go home to the village and what was to stop Philip from seeing her there? Besides, Sophie was fond of her nursemaid and she knew the children would be terribly upset if she left them.

She had clung to the thought that when Philip went away the romance would die a natural death. Margaret would marry that lad in the village and Philip would resign himself to doing his duty by Alice. Up until now she had felt that surely, as he became involved in his life at Oxford he would forget about the pretty little nursemaid. She had tried to convince herself that when he graduated next year, a more mature man, he would be ready to take up his army career and soon be away from further temptation. Last night's revelation had shocked them all but it had hit Sophie the hardest, knowing what she did about her brother's infatuation. She was still trying to convince herself that was all it was but deep down she knew. Her brother and Margaret were in love.

Sophie felt a cold finger of dread down her spine. Now that he intended to stay at home and take over Robert's role, something dreadful would happen; she just knew it.

After breakfast, Thomas announced

that he had to leave on his parish visits.

'I shall need to take the pony and trap,' he said. 'However, it's a lovely day. I'm sure you and the children will enjoy a walk home across the fields.'

'Nonsense,' Robert said. 'It's too far for the little ones. You must return for them when you have finished your visits. Or we can order the carriage for them, if that is more convenient. Anyway, they must stay a little longer. We have the photographer coming later on for a family portrait. Sophie and the children must be here for that.'

'I don't agree with all this fuss and bother,' Thomas said. 'It's pure vanity.'

'It's all arranged. Jane and I want pictures of the family to take with us when we go abroad. Who knows how long it will be before we see you all again?'

'Oh, please, Thomas ... ' Sophie said.

'Very well, you can stay. I'll come back and fetch you when I've done my visits.'

He left the room without saying goodbye, obviously in a bad mood. Sophie sighed. How could she speak to her husband about something as sensitive as her concern about her brother's behaviour, when he was so set in his beliefs of what was right and wrong?

Philip laughed. 'Oh well. It looks as if the family portrait will be missing one member.'

There was a knock on the dining room and Margaret entered with the children, all dressed in their best with shiny faces and hair neatly combed.

'They're all ready, Ma'am,' Margaret said, studiously avoiding looking at Philip.

'The man will be here in a few minutes,' Robert said. 'Let's all go out on to the terrace and line up.'

'Are you sure it's warm enough, Robert?' Jane asked. 'I don't want you getting a chill.'

'Perhaps in the library then?' Sophie suggested.

The photographs took all morning. The photographer was patience itself, posing the whole family, the grandparents sitting, the sons and daughter behind them and the children ranged in front.

'Stand quite still,' he ordered, diving under the black cloth and starting to count.

As he re-emerged they all moved and sighed with relief, but it was not over yet. 'One more,' the man said.

When a further group picture had been taken, Robert insisted on one of himself with Jane, then he had to have one of the Blandford children. 'And what about a portrait of Sophie on her own?' he said.

Sophie protested but the rest of the family insisted and she forced herself to sit still for a further few minutes. She held herself stiffly, gazing into space, her thoughts still on her brother while the photographer disappeared under the black cloth once more.

As he finished and began packing up his equipment, the children begged to be allowed to go and play outside.

'Stay close to the house though,' Sophie said. 'Father will be back soon and we mustn't keep him waiting.'

12

Jo woke early and turned over in bed to see that Edward was still sleeping. After she'd tucked him in last night she had looked in on the girls but both of them had been fast asleep. So what had disturbed him — and her? Had she just dreamt she'd heard a child crying?

She slipped out of bed, anxious not to wake her nephew after his disturbed night. There was no rush, today being Saturday. She could hear Rose and Amy giggling. At least they had settled in OK and did not seem to be too upset by their mother's absence.

She left the girls to their game and pulled on her dressing gown. Lucy would not surface for ages and Jo relished the peace and quiet before the start of another hectic day. Downstairs she filled the kettle for her early morning tea. Glancing out of the window, she noticed that the ground had been disturbed at the far edge of the overgrown terrace. Lucy's attempts at archaeology, she thought.

'*Why don't they leave things alone, let them rest?*' The thought popped into her head, startling her. Where had that come from? She made the tea and sat at the table, cradling the mug in her hands to warm them. Bright September sunshine flooded the kitchen but she still felt cold. She really must phone the heating engineers.

Her thoughts returned to the photos she had found at the Manor and she went to get the scanned copies out of her bag, peering at the faded and watermarked image of the house. The words St Mark's Rectory were quite clear though. It was definitely the original house. She would show it to Lucy later, although at the moment her own interest in finding out the history of her house had somewhat abated since her daughter had shown such enthusiasm for the project in front of Jack. The thought of him having an excuse to spend more time here unsettled her.

Hearing movement from upstairs, she took her mug to the sink, and readied herself for the day. Another glance out of the window at the disturbed ground made her shiver. What would they find? I don't want to know, she thought. I'll take the kids out somewhere and leave Lucy to get on with it.

*   *   *

Despite her desire to get out of the house and away from an atmosphere that was becoming increasingly oppressive, Jo's plans were thrown into disarray when Lucy announced that Jack was coming round to carry on the excavations in the garden.

'Ooh, goody,' Rosie exclaimed. 'Will he put the swing up for us? He promised.'

'I don't think so,' Lucy said. 'I don't think you've met Jack yet.'

Odd, thought Jo. Who else could it have been?

'Besides,' Lucy continued, 'Mum's taking you out and we'll be busy.'

'Can't we help?' Edward asked. 'I like digging.'

'Stop pestering,' Jo said. 'We're going out. I thought we'd go to the Roman Palace.' Suddenly she couldn't wait to get away from the house.

'I want to stay here,' Edward said.

'Me too,' Amy said.

'Please can't we stay? We've been to the Roman Palace lots of times,' Rosie chimed in.

'But you like it there!'

'Let them stay, Mum. If you want to go out, I'll keep an eye on them,' Lucy offered.

Jo hesitated, then said, 'OK, if you're sure. I need to do some shopping anyway.' Perhaps it would be a good idea if the children were around when Jack turned up. If he did have designs on Lucy it would put a damper on his plans.

★　★　★

Jo wandered round the supermarket throwing things at random into the trolley, and trying to rationalise her feelings. Her enthusiasm when she'd moved in and started on the renovations had been overwhelming. She loved the place and couldn't wait till everything was finished and she could settle down to enjoying her new life. She had also looked forward to having her sister's children there. The New Rectory was the sort of house that really needed a family.

So why had her feelings changed since the kids arrived? It must be the problems with Edward, she thought. Still, this morning he'd seemed none the worse for his disturbed night and had even been looking forward to helping with the 'dig', as Lucy called it.

'It'll be like *Time Team*,' he had said, pulling on his wellingtons and rummaging in the box of toys which Jo had brought from Liz's house. Grabbing his little seaside spade, he had rushed out into the garden.

Jo smiled. Kids were so resilient, as long as they felt secure and loved. She finished the shopping and decided to go for a coffee before going home, confident that the children were being well looked after.

As she sipped her drink she found herself going over the strange things that had happened since moving in. There was Lucy's fascination with the graveyard, the sounds of singing and crying she and the children had heard, and the coincidence of finding the photo of the house among the papers at the Manor. Then there was Edward's uncharacteristic behaviour, not to mention the chill in certain parts of the house.

Lucy had jokingly suggested that the house was haunted but Jo had roundly dismissed such an idea. She didn't believe in such things. There was a rational explanation for everything. The weird sounds were probably just the wind blowing through the trees; Lucy had always been interested in history, and it was inevitable she would be curious about the remains of the original rectory; Edward was upset about his mother being in hospital; and the heating engineers had obviously botched the installation of the new system. With that thought, she got out her mobile to phone them. It went to voicemail and she left a message explaining the problem and asking if someone could come and look at it as soon as possible.

As she drove home the thought of that photograph of her house kept intruding. Something about it nagged at her. Why had it been among those at the Manor? She shook it off, deciding that when she got to work on Monday she would delve into the archives and keep looking until she found an explanation. Clive hadn't seemed interested, but he probably couldn't help anyway. Having worked for several weeks now on the family documents, she probably knew more about the history of the Manor and its former inhabitants than he did. He might have a clue about the mysterious Sophie, though. She must be related to the Graylings, perhaps a cousin or something.

She parked the car in the drive and

called out for someone to help her bring the bags indoors. There was no reply and she guessed they were having too much fun in the back garden to take any notice. Sighing, she went in and dumped the bags on the kitchen table.

She opened the back door and called, 'Lucy, kids, where are you?'

Edward's spade was stuck at an angle in a pile of earth but there was no one there. Where had they got to?

Puzzled, she went out into the back garden. Surely Lucy hadn't taken her cousins out somewhere without phoning or leaving a note. They must be around here somewhere.

She walked down to the end of the garden and through the tangle of shrubbery towards the gap in the hedge, calling as she went. The wind rustled the few remaining leaves on the trees with a sound like a sigh. She stopped, her head cocked to one side. Yes it did sound a bit like music, she thought, smiling at her foolishness. But as she was about to turn away, she stopped. It *was* music

— singing. And it was coming from the churchyard.

She pushed her way through the hedge and saw Jack sitting on a table-like tombstone, strumming a guitar while Lucy and her cousins held hands and danced to the music. The two girls were laughing and chanting the old nursery rhyme, 'Ladybird, ladybird, fly away home'. Edward didn't look as if he was enjoying himself though, and when he spotted Jo he ran to her, throwing his arms round her legs and clinging on.

'You're home, Auntie Jo. Can we go indoors now?' he asked.

'What on earth are you up to?' Jo asked, glaring at Lucy. 'This is hardly a suitable playground for the children.'

'We were playing hide and seek,' Rosie said. 'It was fun.'

'Well, I think you'd better go inside now and have some lunch. Run along.' Joanne turned to Lucy. 'Where's Ben? I thought he was going to come over.'

'He didn't turn up,' Lucy said. 'It doesn't matter. Jack was here and we

202

found something, didn't we?'

'Very interesting, Mrs Mason,' Jack said, leaping off the tombstone and slinging his guitar across his shoulder. 'Come on, I'll show you.'

'Not now. I must get the children's lunch. You are staying, I take it?'

'No, thanks. I've got stuff to do.' He dropped a brief kiss on Lucy's cheek. 'See you,' he said, disappearing through the gap in the hedge.

Jo couldn't hide her relief and Lucy turned to her, a fierce scowl on her face.

'I know you don't like him, Mum, but do you have to make it so obvious?'

'I don't know what you mean,' Jo said. 'I do know that I don't like you messing about in the churchyard. I don't want the children in here again. We must block up that gap in the hedge.'

'Don't be silly, Mum. There's nothing here to hurt them. It's just an adventure playground to them.'

'I just don't understand your fascination with the place, that's all.' She pointed to the row of small graves which they

203

had noticed on their first visit here. 'And what is it about these graves? I've noticed you seem to be particularly interested in them.'

Lucy's eyes suddenly welled with tears.

'I don't know, Mum. I just feel so sad whenever I think of them. Three little children, the same ages as my cousins. I know it was all a long time ago, but I can't help wondering what happened to them.'

Joanne put her arm round her daughter.

'You big softy, you,' she said, her anger evaporating. She gave her an affectionate squeeze. 'Come on. Lunch.'

'Wait, Mum. Look.' Lucy pointed to the graves where she had scraped away the lichen to reveal more of the names they had seen earlier. 'There's an Edward, aged eight, the same as our Edward,' she said with a catch in her voice.

Joanne glanced down and gasped. With the lichen scraped away, she could now make out the whole surname. 'Blandford' — the name on the photograph she'd found at Grayling Manor. She recalled the beautiful but rather solemn face of the young woman called Sophie Blandford. So who was she, and what was her connection with both the Rectory and the Manor?

Lucy looked at her mum, surprised by her reaction. 'What is it?' she asked.

'Look,' said Jo, fishing the scanned copies of the photos out of her bag. 'I found these. I've been meaning to show you.'

'St Mark's Rectory ... Is that our house?' said Lucy, then, 'And Sophie Blandford? I wonder what connection she has to our three little children? Where in the house were these hiding, Mum?'

'That's just it,' said Jo. 'I didn't find the photos here — they're from Grayling Manor.'

13

The next day the children were awake early, excited about going home. Liz had come out of hospital the previous day and couldn't wait to have them back.

Jo had been a bit worried that she wouldn't be able to cope but Mike was due home and Liz wanted her family all together.

'I don't blame you,' Jo said when she dropped the children off later that morning. 'But don't go overdoing it. And if you need anything, ring me. Lucy or I will be over like a shot.'

'You've already done so much,' Liz said. 'I can't thank you enough.'

'That's what sisters are for,' Jo said, giving her a hug. She put the shepherd's pie she'd made for them into the fridge and made her sister a cup of tea before leaving.

As she drove back to the New Rectory

she felt a little sad. She'd miss having those lively kids around. And when Lucy went off to Exeter next week she'd be all alone. Not for the first time Jo felt a little flicker of doubt about the house. What on earth had possessed her to take on such a burden?

She pulled up in the driveway, noticing an unfamiliar vehicle in the lane. To her dismay, Jack's van was there too. Thank goodness Lucy would soon be away from what Jo saw as a disturbing influence on her daughter.

A voice called from over the hedge as she started up the path and she turned to see a familiar face peering at her through the foliage.

'Oh, it's you, Father Tim. I didn't recognise your car.' Jo hadn't seen him since that earlier encounter, when she had first stumbled across the house.

'I had hoped to see you at the service this morning,' he said.

'I'm sorry, I didn't realise there was a service today.' Joanne would have gone, if only out of curiosity.

'Once a month. Only a handful of congregation, but we have to do it.'

Jo felt uncomfortable conversing through a gap in the hedge and thought about inviting him in. But before she could say anything, he said, 'I got the feeling when we spoke before that you were interested in the history of the church. Would you like me to show you round before I lock up? If you have time, that is.'

After a brief hesitation, she agreed, although she ought to go in and see what her daughter and that young man were up to, she thought. But a few minutes wouldn't make any difference.

She hurried round to the lych-gate, declining to squeeze through the gap in the hedge. Father Tim opened the door and stood back to let her in. The musty smell of combined dust, damp and old hymn books greeted her and she wrinkled her nose, coughing a little. Thank goodness I didn't sit through a service in here, she thought.

But, as she looked around, she was able to ignore the air of neglect and take in the lovely stained-glass window at the east end, something she'd never noticed from the outside, and the stone font. It was badly worn but she could make out some of the carved figures round the outside.

'It's Saxon,' Father Tim said. 'And the rood screen is 14th century.'

'It's lovely,' Joanne said, walking up the aisle to examine it more closely. 'Such a pity the church is so seldom used.'

'I agree. The sad thing is, it won't be in use at all for much longer. The church commissioners won't pay for the upkeep. Besides, the new church in town gets a good turnout each week — our funds should be invested there.'

'Makes sense, I suppose.' Jo wandered into one of the side aisles and looked at the plaques on the wall. Near the pulpit was a wooden board inscribed with the names of previous rectors, dating back to the 1300s. As her eye ran down the list, she gasped.

'Rev. Thomas Blandford, 1879–1890,' she whispered. She put a hand to her chest, breathing quickly.

She turned to Father Tim. 'Do you know anything about the previous rectors?' she asked.

'Not really.' He noticed which name she was pointing to and nodded. 'Oh yes, that one. His children are buried in the churchyard. I'm not sure what happened. Some contagious illness I expect. Cholera, typhoid. Common enough in those days.'

But Jo knew there was more to it than that — how, she wasn't sure. It was just a feeling. She shook her head. She'd been having too many of these feelings lately.

As she followed Father Tim around the little church she couldn't concentrate on what he was saying, her mind full of the strange coincidences that kept cropping up. Of course, if she hadn't been working at the Manor and delving into the Grayling history, she wouldn't have given the name another thought. But there was definitely a connection between the previous inhabitants of her house and her boss's family.

Almost without realising it she found

herself back in the church porch and Father Tim was saying, 'I really must lock up now but if you want to look round when I've more time, just give me a ring.'

He handed her a card and she thanked him.

'I might take you up on that,' she said. 'It was most interesting.' But she was only speaking out of politeness. Suddenly, she couldn't wait to get away.

She heard laughter from the back garden and saw Jack splitting logs while Lucy watched. She went indoors and made drinks, then opened the back door and called to them.

'You must be freezing out there. I've made hot chocolate. Come inside.'

'Thanks, Mum.' Lucy turned with an armful of logs. 'Shall I bring these in or put them in the shed?'

'Bring them in. I'm going to light the wood burner later on.' She smiled at Jack. 'You too, Jack. You deserve a rest.'

She still couldn't take to the young man but she couldn't deny that he was a hard worker and he seemed to enjoy helping out in the garden. Jo wondered if he'd still be so keen once her daughter went away to university. To her relief, Lucy didn't seem to be encouraging him, treating him with a casual camaraderie. And she was still seeing quite a lot of Ben too.

Jo poured the drinks and sat down at the kitchen table with them. 'It's very good of you to help out, Jack,' she said.

'Glad to, Mrs Mason. I love working outdoors, and helping to get this place into shape is a real challenge. Besides, I've got interested in all this history stuff. Lucy was telling me she wants to find out a bit about the people who lived here before. Something about a connection to the Manor?'

'I think I've caught Mum's bug,' Lucy said. 'I just love delving around in old documents and stuff.'

'I'm sure there is a connection with the Manor,' said Jo. 'There must be, or else why would that photo of the rectory be among their archives? It's such a coincidence that I bought this house without knowing about any of it.' Joanne almost went on to mention her conversation with Father Tim, but stopped herself. Lucy might start on again about the children's graves and she didn't want her getting upset again.

'I spoke to my gran about the work you're doing at the Manor,' Jack said. 'Her family have lived in the village for generations. In fact, her grandmother used to work up there.'

'Really?' Jo leaned forward, forgetting about the Blandfords for a moment, her eyes alight with interest.

'She said there was some scandal way back. She wasn't sure what actually happened. Anyway, after that the Grayling family lost their money, the house fell into disrepair and, as you know, the family almost died out.'

Jo wondered how much Clive knew about this. He had never given any indication that there was a scandal attached to the Grayling name. Perhaps the Canadian side of the family hadn't known about it. How would he feel if, in the course of her research, she discovered something? Would he want it covered up or feel it was all part of the colourful history of Grayling Manor? It would certainly make an entertaining story to tell when the house was finally open to the public, but would Clive agree? Perhaps he wouldn't want a family scandal aired in public.

Lost in thought, she almost missed Jack's next words.

'We've found more signs of the fire that destroyed the previous house,' he said. 'It must have been a huge building originally. There are piles of old burnt tiles and bricks at the end of the garden. They were almost buried under that jungle of shrubs.'

'People had big families and servants in those days,' Joanne said. 'And vicarages were always large, like that one on the main road — you know, the one that's been turned into flats. I expect that's what would have happened to this if it hadn't caught fire.'

Lucy finished her chocolate and stood up.

'Come on, Jack, more work to do.'

He laughed. 'OK, bossy-boots.'

Jo rinsed the mugs under the tap and followed them outside. She noted with approval the big pile of logs, the result of lopping off the overhanging branches of the large sycamore which had almost taken over the end of the garden. When Jo noticed the swing that hung from one of the sturdier branches, she thought to herself that it looked as though it had always been there.

Jack and Lucy had also cut back a sprawling lilac bush and several other unidentifiable shrubs. The branches were piled in the middle of what would eventually become the lawn.

'I suppose we'll have to burn this lot,' Jo said.

'We could save it all for Guy Fawkes night, have a party,' Lucy said. 'I can come home for the weekend.'

'I don't know.' Jo wasn't really keen on the idea.

'Go on, Mum. It'll be fun. We could have Auntie Liz and the cousins over. The kids would love it.'

'A good way to get rid of the rubbish,' Jack said. 'There's all that stuff in the old shed too, not to mention the remains of the shed itself.'

'I suppose so.' Jo had been thinking of hiring a skip but a fire would save the expense. 'OK then. But we must make sure it's safe if we're going to have the children here.' She turned to go back indoors.

'Wait, Mum. Come and see what we found.' Lucy led her down the garden and pointed to a pile of rubble which had, until now, been hidden beneath the tangle of greenery. 'I wonder why this wasn't all cleared away when they rebuilt the house?' she said.

'Perhaps they ran out of money,' Jo said. It seemed the most likely explanation. She pulled at the tangle of ivy which almost smothered a low flint wall. 'This wasn't part of the house though. Looks as if it might have been stables or a carriage house.'

'But some of the bricks look burnt,'

216

Lucy said, pointing to the tumble of blackened masonry. 'I thought it was the house which caught fire.' She kicked at the heap of rubble, revealing shards of coloured glass which sparked miniature rainbows in the weak autumn sun.

Jo picked up a fragment of blue glass, holding it up to the light.

'I recognise this. It's from the house,' she said.

'What do you mean?' Lucy asked.

'The picture I showed you, of the old house. It had a window over the porch, like a church window.'

'But that was in black and white. How could you tell it was stained glass?'

'I don't know — it's just a feeling.'

Jo threw the fragment down on the ground, rubbing her hand against her skirt. She shivered.

'We'd better get rid of this before the children come again. Don't want them getting hurt,' she said.

She hurried into the house, feeling a little faint, and sank into a chair. What was wrong with her? It wasn't like her to get bad vibes, as Lucy called them, not from something as innocent as picking up a shard of glass, anyway. She shivered again and shook her head. I just got cold out there, she told herself. But suddenly she was reluctant to delve into the history of the New Rectory any further. The house, which had seemed the answer to her dreams only a few months ago, now seemed alien and unwelcoming. But what could she do? There was no way she could afford to move again.

Lucy and Jack burst through the back door laughing, each carrying an armful of logs. As they stacked them in the alcove alongside the wood burner, Jo's feelings of foreboding receded. With the young people horsing around, the place seemed warmer somehow, more friendly. But soon Lucy would be going away and she would be on her own.

I knew I'd miss her, Jo thought, but I didn't bank on feeling quite so miserable about it. She looked round the room, wondering what had possessed her to buy such a big house when she'd always known she would be spending so much time alone here.

It was times like this when she most missed Tom. How much more pleasure she would take in her new home if there was someone to share it with. But it wasn't Tom she was thinking of. Unbidden, a picture of Clive Grayling rose in her mind, his dark hair flopping over his forehead, his expression intent as he studied the old archives discovered in his family home. She shrugged the thought away. It was too soon to think about a new relationship. Besides, she wouldn't dream of doing anything to upset Lucy while she was still grieving for her father.

But would she be upset? she wondered. Lucy had grown up a lot since getting her place at university. And besides, she would soon be making her own way in life. Would she really begrudge her mother a chance at happiness?

Jo gave herself a little shake. What was she thinking of? Clive had never shown any interest in her other than as an employee, although she did think that they were becoming close friends. But that was due to their shared interest in the Grayling Manor project. Jo laughed. Her thoughts were getting out of hand.

And as for her recent feelings about the house, she was just being silly. She loved the place — she really did. It was great having the extra room so that her nieces and nephew could come and stay. She had enjoyed looking after them while Liz was in hospital, despite Edward's nightmares and the mad scramble to get them to school and herself to work on time.

Then there was the convenience of being so close to the Manor. She was now cycling to work each day and hoped to carry on doing so until the weather changed. And she felt so much fitter not using the car so much. Yes, she told herself, living at the New Rectory was much more convenient than the previous house, where she'd had to leave home each morning half an hour earlier than was really necessary to avoid the traffic, and where her sleep was constantly disturbed by the late-night drinkers leaving the pub on the corner.

Jack and Lucy had gone into the garden again and Jo listened to them laughing. She resolved to tell them to stop exploring the foundations of the old stable building. The fire was history. This house — her house — with its new kitchen and bathroom was a home for the twenty-first century. There was no way, whatever had happened before the fire, that the ghosts of the past could have lingered on. But still, a feeling of foreboding swept over her.

14

Jo leaned back in her chair and stretched her arms above her head. She had been typing for what seemed like hours and she knew she should have taken a break earlier. Immersing herself in the Grayling family tree had served to take her mind off her foolish thoughts about her own house and its history. A fascinating story was emerging and she couldn't wait to add all the new strands to the database

She went to the window and stood watching the men at work. It was cold and windy but at least the rain had held off and they were able to get on with the outside repairs. She had assumed that once the roof was made weatherproof, they would start on the inside. But the stone parapet around the tower and the pediment over the main door were crumbling away. A specialist had been brought in to restore it all and at last the

Manor was beginning to look as she had imagined it had in its heyday.

She had hoped for a glimpse of Clive but she hadn't seen him so far today. He must be working outside. He hadn't joined her for their usual morning coffee and she felt a pang of disappointment. She enjoyed their chats and had begun to look forward to him coming into the kitchen and leaning against the worktop while they waited for the kettle to boil. She flushed a little, remembering Lucy teasing her about him. But there was nothing in it, she told herself. Besides, their conversations were all about the Grayling archives.

Lost in thought, she started when the door opened behind her, feeling the heat rising up her face as Clive spoke. She hoped her blush didn't reveal her thoughts about him.

'I thought you'd gone,' he said. 'I know you're keen, but it's way past your home time.'

'I know.' She took a deep breath and turned to face him. 'This stuff is so

223

interesting I quite lost track of time. I suppose I'd better get off though.'

'How's your sister doing, now she's home from the hospital? Is she OK?'

'She's fine — just gone back to work in fact.'

'I hope she's not overdoing it so soon after her operation.' Clive put his hand on her shoulder. 'You too, Jo. You've done such a good job here — over and above actually. Sure you wouldn't like a few days off.'

'That's good of you, Clive. It's OK though. I'm fine.' She switched off the computer and picked up her bag.

'I've just remembered — I have something to show you. Still, it can wait till tomorrow.'

Jo laughed. 'You mustn't do that. Now you've got me all curious.'

He just grinned. 'Well, you'll have to wait and see. Now, get off home.' As she reached the door he said, 'And by the way — don't wear anything decent to work tomorrow.'

When she started to ask why he just

shook his head.

'You'll find out,' he said with a grin.

★ ★ ★

As she cycled along the lane, enjoying the crisp autumn day, Jo puzzled over Clive's parting words. Perhaps he was going to let her up in the attics at last. There were still parts of the rambling old mansion that she hadn't yet seen and she was dying to explore. He had insisted it was too dangerous, especially after he'd put his foot through the floor that time. Often when he came into the library with boxes of papers and old photos, he'd have cobwebs in his hair and his face would be streaked with dust. Fortunately there had been no further accidents but she did worry about him when hours passed and he did not appear.

It had been such a shock when he had staggered through the door, covered in dirt, bruised and bleeding from cuts. It had made her realise how much she was beginning to care for him. He could have been badly hurt.

She tried not to think about it and instead, focused on his last words to her. She was consumed with curiosity. She couldn't wait to start rummaging around among the trunks and boxes that were still stored in the attics.

Although Clive shared his discoveries with her, it didn't have the same excitement as it would if she found something herself. That brought her back to her earlier thought, and this time she couldn't push it to the back of her mind. These days she had to admit she was thinking more about Clive than she was about Tom.

She still missed her husband of course, and now, although Lucy came home some weekends, she often felt lonely. She missed having someone to talk to about her plans for the house and garden, and those little everyday problems which faded into insignificance when shared. Could Clive fill that gap in her life? It was true they mostly talked about the progress of the Manor's restoration and her work on the archives. Perhaps it was just their shared interests which made her look forward to going into work each day.

A long lonely evening stretched in front of her and she decided not to spend it mulling over these disturbing thoughts. She would pop over to see Liz, have a couple of glasses of wine and a gossip, try to put the world to rights as they usually did.

And she would put Clive Grayling right out of her head. After all, if he was beginning to have romantic feelings for her — and she was sure he was not, she told herself — how would Lucy feel about someone taking her father's place?

* * *

When she got to Liz's, the children were ready for bed and the cosy chat had to be deferred.

'Read us a story, Auntie Jo,' Amy said, swinging on her aunt's arm. 'Please … '

'Leave your auntie alone. She's had a hard day at work.'

'I don't mind,' Jo said.

'All right — but just one story,' Liz said. 'I'll make some supper and get the wine out, so don't be too long.'

It turned out to be several stories and Amy insisted on 'The Very Hungry Caterpillar' one more time before they settled down to sleep.

Downstairs, Liz looked up with a grin.

'Sorry about that. Still, you managed to escape.'

Jo sank down on the couch. 'I don't mind, really. I enjoy reading to them. Anyway, I think they've settled down now.'

'Good. Now we can have a good old natter. Here, get that down you.' She handed Jo a glass of wine. 'So how're things going?'

'Where do I start?'

'The house first. Is it all done now?'

'Just a few cosmetic touches to go. It's the garden mainly.'

Liz laughed. 'The jungle, you mean.'

'Not quite so much of a jungle now. Lucy and Jack have done wonders. But there's still a lot to do. I want to get rid of some of the trees.'

'Don't you have to get permission from the council to chop mature trees down?'

'I'll contact them tomorrow. But surely they can't refuse. They're blocking the light.'

Liz waved her protest aside. 'Never mind about that — what about the Manor and your dishy boss?'

Jo felt herself flushing.

'He's OK. Not bad as bosses go,' she said, with an attempt at casualness. 'Anyway, it's the job I'm keen on. It's fascinating.'

She told Liz about the photos she'd discovered, and about Sophie Blandford. 'She must be a relative of the Graylings, or why would her photo be among the Manor archives?'

'What does Clive think?'

Jo's hand flew to her mouth. 'I haven't showed it to him. I only pointed out the picture of St Mark's Rectory.'

'How come?'

'I completely forgot about it until just now.'

But even as she spoke, Jo realised that wasn't entirely true. There was something unsettling about that particular picture. For some unknown reason she had been reluctant to speak to Clive about it. She told herself she'd been waiting until she had discovered more about it so that she could tell him the whole story.

Liz topped up her glass. 'So, what about your boss? Come on, tell all.'

'There's nothing to tell. I like him. We get on well. But that's all, Liz.'

Her sister gave a disbelieving laugh.

'I think there's more to it than that. And why not?' She leaned forward and touched Jo's knee. 'You can't go on grieving forever, love. No one thinks you should forget Tom. But you have to start living again.'

'I am. I've moved house, started a new job ... '

'There's more to life than work, Jo.'

'But it's such an interesting job. I've got so wrapped up in it — it's almost as if I've gone back in time. I can almost see the people who lived at the Manor and the lives they led.'

'Have you found out any more about the present Grayling? How he ended up in Canada as the long lost heir?'

Jo laughed. 'You're determined to get me to talk about him, aren't you?'

'Well, you must admit it's intriguing. He turns up out of the blue to claim his inheritance ... '

'Not quite out of the blue. I think the solicitors employed one of those agencies who track down family trees and try to find heirs.'

'What would have happened to the Manor if they hadn't found anyone?'

'I think the government gets it in those cases.'

Liz took a gulp of her wine. 'The government? Well, thank god they found him, then!'

'Apparently, it was his mother who was a Grayling — his surname is actually Wood. It was a condition of inheriting that he took the name Grayling.'

'Can they do that then; make you change your name?'

'Apparently. I seem to remember reading somewhere that Jane Austen's brother had to change his name so that he could inherit the 'big house' as she always called it.'

'But that was two hundred years ago. It seems a bit daft to me,' Liz said.

'I suppose the old man wanted a Grayling to inherit Grayling Manor.' Jo took a sip of wine and put the glass down. 'Anyway, Clive said he's used to it now. And of course, the locals don't know any different.'

'It sounds as if you've been having some cosy chats. It's not all work and no play,' Liz teased.

'Don't be silly, Liz. It just cropped up when we were cataloguing some papers.'

Liz gave a disbelieving snort and leaned forward touch her sister's cheek.

'I do believe you're blushing,' she said.

'Can we change the subject please?' Jo was beginning to get embarrassed and more than a little irritated at her sister's persistence.

'OK. Just one last question. When I

am I going to meet the mysterious Mr Grayling?'

Her daughter had asked the same question when she had phoned the other evening, and Jo had since been contemplating asking Clive to the New Rectory for a meal when Lucy was next home. Trouble was, she hadn't been able to think of a good excuse.

'I'll think about it,' she said. 'Now, let's change the subject. It's half term next week and I'm looking forward to seeing Lucy. I've really missed her.'

For the rest of the evening they talked about the children, and Lucy's progress at university, and Jo was able to put any disturbing thoughts of Clive Grayling out of her mind — for the time being at least.

But after she'd said her goodbyes and a taxi had dropped her home, she was still a little distracted by her sister's earlier remarks. Liz had always been prone to teasing but she had to admit that her references to Clive and the possibility that Jo was beginning to have romantic feelings for him had hit home.

Perhaps it was time to admit that her eagerness to get to the Manor each day had more to do with its owner than with her interest in the Graylings' family history.

15

Jo hung her coat up in the hall and went into the kitchen. It was still cold and she went to check the thermostat. Hadn't she set the heating to come on an hour before she was due home? The place should have warmed up by now. She twiddled the knob to its highest setting but after half an hour there was no change in the temperature.

She sighed. I suppose I'll have to phone the engineer yet again, she thought. Last time he'd come, he'd checked the system thoroughly and assured her there was nothing wrong, but there was obviously still a problem.

She went through to the study and switched on her computer, draping a cardigan round her shoulders and pulling her chair closer to the screen. She would send an email to Lucy bringing her up to date with the latest discoveries at the Manor.

She didn't want to be one of those mums constantly texting and phoning, worrying about what her daughter was up to. But she knew Lucy was interested and these daily reports helped her to keep in touch and made her feel closer to her daughter.

Now that the renovation of the New Rectory was completed there was little for Jo to do in the evenings and when she'd finished the email she pushed her chair back. Her fingers were cold from typing and she went to check the thermostat again. It was still on high and she tapped her foot impatiently. She should have lit the wood burner but it was a bit late for that. Besides, she normally only did so at weekends.

She got out her mobile, keyed in the heating man's number, and left a message.

She switched the television on and surfed through the channels but nothing caught her interest and after a few minutes she switched off and picked up a magazine. It was no good. Her thoughts kept going back to the conversation with

Liz and the realisation that Clive Grayling was becoming more to her than just a boss.

She stood up and paced the room. This was silly. She was behaving like a giddy teenager. It was late and she ought to go to bed but she knew that she wouldn't sleep. Perhaps if she did some online research it would take her mind off these disturbing thoughts.

No, she told herself, I've been working on the computer all day. I'll go cross-eyed if I look at that screen any more.

But the Grayling family history was so interesting, especially as her latest research seemed to be revealing a connection with her house.

She took the scanned photo of the Rectory out of her bag, holding it up to the light to try and make out the fuzzy details. It showed a larger house than the present building but it was undoubtedly the one that had formerly occupied this plot. The church could be seen in the background and that tree in the churchyard, a huge cedar of Lebanon, was surely the same one that shaded a large part of her present garden.

There must be a connection — but what? She replaced the picture in her bag and stood up. Time for bed. As she went to turn out the light she heard a faint sound. It was coming from outside. It sounded like music. Was there something on in the church? It wasn't used regularly but Father Tim had told her that occasionally one of the local groups would put on a concert there. That was usually during festival week though, Jo thought. Besides, it was much too late to still be going on. She switched the light off and went over to the window, pulling the curtain aside and peering out into the dark garden. There was not a glimmer of light anywhere — there were no street lights in Church Lane anyway. But neither could she see anything through the trees that partially screened the church.

As she turned away a sudden gust of wind stirred the branches. Jo was not usually a nervous person. Even before Tom's death she had often been alone in the house when he was away on business and she had never minded. But since moving here she had become more sensitive to odd noises and weird happenings, such as the unexplained temperature changes in the house.

She realised she'd been holding her breath and now she gave a little laugh. It was only the wind, she told herself, shrugging her shoulders and going upstairs. In her room she turned the radio on, tuning it to Classic FM. That would shut out any noises from outside.

As she settled down to sleep, she deliberately turned her thoughts to the documents she had been cataloguing that day and made a mental list of where to start when she reached the Manor next day.

★   ★   ★

To her surprise she slept dreamlessly and woke refreshed, eager to start the next stage of her research. She pulled the curtain aside and looked out into the garden. Of course, there was nothing to see beyond the stretch of lawn and the tangle of shrubbery at the far end. The swing that had been put up for Liz's children moved lazily in the breeze, issuing a faint creaking. That must have been what she'd heard last night. Anything more sinister was all in her imagination, fired up by speculation about the history of her house and its connection with Grayling Manor. How could she possibly have dreamt when she took the job at the Manor and moved in here that the two houses would become so bound up together? It all added to the interest of her job of course, but she couldn't help an uneasy feeling that the connections might turn out to be something she'd rather not know about.

When she got to work and entered the library she found a new pile of documents on the table under the window. Some looked extremely old, the pages mildewed, their corners looking as if they had been chewed by mice. She pulled on a pair of cotton gloves and drew them towards her. Fascinating as the contents of these old documents were, she still sometimes felt reluctant to handle those which were not only dirty, but smelled damp and mouldy too. But it was all part of the job and she took a deep breath, forcing herself to separate them.

She noted that they were much older than anything she'd handled previously and, within minutes, the emerging story of the 18th century Graylings had her completely engrossed and she didn't notice the passing time until Clive came in bearing two steaming mugs of coffee.

'How's it going?' he asked, making her jump.

She turned to face him, laughing nervously.

'You nearly gave me a heart attack,' she protested.

'Sorry. I thought you heard me come in.' He set the mugs down on the table. 'We'll just have our coffee and then it's time for the tour.'

Jo had completely forgotten that he had a surprise in store for her.

'Attics or cellars?' she asked.

'First I want to show you this,' he said, unrolling a sheet of parchment. 'These are plans for an extension to the house, when they added the towers and the front portico.'

'I know it was originally a much older building. You can tell from kitchen and your study.'

'It's even older than I thought,' Clive said. 'Down in the cellars there are stone arches and pillars — obviously medieval, almost like a church crypt.'

'It looks like they added a whole new house on the front of the old one,' Jo said, poring over the old document. 'And I've just started to decipher this.' She showed him a ledger with mouse-nibbled pages.

'As far as I can make out this is the estimate for the cost of building. See.' She pointed to the list of figures. 'Materials, labourers' wages and the architect's fee.'

Clive laughed. 'Wish it only cost that much nowadays. The rate things are going I could run out of money.'

Jo looked dismayed.

'Oh, I do hope not. You've worked so hard.'

'I've applied for a heritage grant, and if that's accepted I should just about manage.'

'Good luck with that, then.'

Clive smiled and put his hand on her shoulder.

'Don't worry. You'll still have a job. I couldn't manage without you now.' He drained his coffee, then said, 'Let's go and explore the foundations of Grayling Manor.'

At the top of the stairs leading down to the cellars, he took her hand.

'Be careful, the steps can be a bit slippery.'

Jo was glad of his support as he guided her down the curving stone steps — or was there another reason she found herself enjoying the warmth of the hand in hers? She could scarcely take in what he was saying as he led her through a labyrinth of cellars deep under the house.

★ ★ ★

'That was amazing, thank you,' she said, as they reached the end of the tour and found themselves back in the Great Hall. 'Now, I suppose I'd better finish what I was doing.'

'No rush,' he said with a smile.

'There is if you want to open early next year. There's loads more to go through yet.'

'Oh, what did your daughter make of the photo of St Mark's Rectory, by the way? Weird, isn't it,' Clive said. 'I mean, you coming to work for me and moving into the New Rectory around the same time, and then finding that.'

'She was as intrigued as I am. She's inherited my love of history. Or just my nosiness, perhaps!'

Clive laughed, and stood up.

'Better get on. I've got a lot to do as well.'

When he'd gone, she sighed. She was beginning to realise that what she wanted was a more tangible connection with Clive Grayling than sharing a bit of ancient history.

16

Jo poured herself a glass of wine and spread the scanned photos out on her coffee table. In addition to the photos of Sophie and the former rectory, she had discovered a group photo, which she knew must have been taken at the Manor. She recognised the marble fireplace behind the group — it was the same fireplace that graced the room where she now spent her working day.

They all looked so stiff and formal, even the children. But then, in the early days of photography, the sitter had to keep very still for several minutes until the photographer told them they could relax. How things have changed, she thought, smiling at the thought of Lucy and her 'selfies'. How many of the thousands of photographs being taken today would still be studied in a hundred years' time?

She could recognise Sophie from the portrait she had already studied, and those must be her parents, the older couple seated in the centre. There was another young woman in the photo and two handsome young men. Was one of them Sophie's husband? Three children were posed in front of the adults — a boy and two girls, each about the same age that Liz's children were now. Was that Edward and his two sisters? This must have been taken shortly before they died, she realised.

A lump came to her throat at the thought of those small graves in the churchyard only yards from where she was now sitting. She shivered as the similarity of the Blandford children's names to those of her nephew and nieces forced itself upon her. Combined with so many recent incidents — her daughter's sleep-walking in the churchyard, the coldness of the house, not to mention the connections with the New Rectory and Grayling Manor — she couldn't help feeling that there might be something in Lucy's assertion that the place was haunted.

She pushed the photographs aside and took a large mouthful of wine. This is silly, she told herself. I definitely don't believe in all that nonsense. It's just my imagination being stirred up by being so involved in the Grayling family history.

She picked up her mobile and called her sister's number. A chat with Liz always helped. She would laugh off her concerns and make her see how daft she was being.

To her relief, Liz answered straight away and launched straight into an account of what the children had been doing at school.

'They've no sooner gone back after half term and all that Halloween nonsense than they're talking about Guy Fawkes,' she said. 'They want a party — and fireworks. Well, you know how I feel about that, and our garden's far too small for a bonfire anyway. But the usual organised display near here has been cancelled, and I don't know of any others.'

'Actually, Lucy suggested a while ago that we do a bonfire for Guy Fawkes, to get rid of all the cuttings from the garden. Plus that tumbledown shed is full of junk we could burn. I've been thinking about having a house-warming party too, so why don't we combine the two?' Jo said. 'I'll do the food. Mike's due to be home, right? He can be in charge of fireworks. Not too many and none of the really dangerous ones, of course,' she added hastily as Liz was about to protest.

'Just us?' Liz asked.

'Lucy will be home too, and she'll want Ben to come; Jack as well I suppose.' Jo paused. 'And I thought I'd ask Clive.'

Liz chuckled. 'I knew it. You *are* interested in him.'

'He's my boss, and a friend — nothing more,' Jo said.

'OK, I believe you.'

'I've been thinking of asking him over for a meal so that I can show him the church. I'm sure the former rector is a relative of his family.' Before Liz could interrupt with another comment about her interest in Clive, Jo continued hastily, 'It's not what you think, really. The only reason I haven't invited him before is I didn't want him to get the wrong idea. But a party with lots of other people here ... '

'All right, I understand,' Liz said, laughing. 'So when do you want to do this party, then?'

'Well, November 5th is on a Saturday and Lucy will be home that weekend, so we can have it on the actual day.'

'OK. I'll help you with the food. We'll get together soon and work out what we need. I won't say anything to the kids yet, I don't want them getting over-excited.'

Jo switched off her phone and sat back in the chair, feeling better after talking to her sister. A party was something to look forward to and a houseful of people would help to dispel the atmosphere that was making her so uneasy. Since Lucy had gone away, she was gradually beginning to admit to herself that the New Rectory wasn't quite the house of her dreams. It really wasn't suitable for someone living alone. She sighed and closed her eyes. As she drifted off to sleep, the faint sound of children's voices singing impinged on her consciousness and she jerked upright. She had been dreaming — hadn't she?

Silence surrounded her and she stood up. She must have imagined it, a half-dream brought on by thinking about the party and the thought of her sister's children dancing round the bonfire. But why would such an image cause that strange hollow feeling in the pit of her stomach?

17

1890

It was a cold, crisp autumn day and the children ran out to the garden after their lessons, delighted to be free from the schoolroom.

'Come on, you two. Let's start building the bonfire,' Edward said. 'Uncle Philip will be coming over tomorrow for Guy Fawkes Night.'

Edward went to the end of the garden where Bill, the gardener, had been cutting back the shrubbery which was encroaching on to the lawn. He grabbed one of the branches and pulled at it, biting his lip in determination. It suddenly came free and he staggered backwards, scowling at Amelia as she started to laugh.

'What do you think you're doing?'

The harsh voice brought Edward up short and he dropped the branch.

'We're making a bonfire, Father.'

'No. I forbid it. I've already told you — no bonfires,' said Thomas.

'It's for Guy Fawkes night, Father. The Gunpowder Plot.'

'It's pagan nonsense. I won't have it.'

'But we've been learning about Guy Fawkes and how he wanted to blow up the Houses of Parliament. Mama told us they passed a law to say we should always celebrate him getting caught.' He started to recite the old rhyme. 'Remember, remember, the fifth of November ... '

'Quiet, boy,' Thomas snapped.

Edward's face fell and Thomas softened his voice. 'Edward, my son, I'm pleased you are learning your lessons so well, but I still say no bonfire in the garden. It's far too dangerous.'

Edward pouted but he knew that once his father had made up his mind there was little chance of him changing it. Still, perhaps Uncle Philip could talk him round, the boy thought, hopefully.

★ ★ ★

The next day Philip arrived while the children were still at their lessons. He knocked on the library door and opened it.

'Sorry to disturb you, Sophie,' he said. 'I just called to tell you I have now formally left Oxford. I won't be going back for the rest of the term.'

'So, you really meant what you said about taking over the running of the estate?' Sophie said.

'Of course. Robert and Jane leave for the south of France next week.'

'I hope you've made the right decision, Philip. It's a big step.'

Philip frowned. 'You don't think I'm capable of it, do you?'

'Of course I do.'

The children had been quiet during this exchange, apparently busy with the maps they were drawing and colouring in. Now, Amelia looked up, a huge smile on her face.

'Does that mean you will be staying here, not going away?' she asked.

Philip nodded.

'Oh, goody,' Rosalind squealed. 'You can come over and play with us every day.'

'I'm afraid your uncle will be far too busy with his work on the estate,' Sophie said. She hoped that was true. It wouldn't do to have him popping over to the Rectory too often. For she knew in her heart that, although he loved the children and genuinely enjoyed their company, that would not be his main reason for visiting. And seeing more of Margaret would only increase the risk of someone discovering their liaison.

'That's true,' Philip said. 'But I'll visit whenever I have time.'

'You'll have time to help us with the bonfire though, won't you?' Edward asked.

'Now then, Edward, you know very well your father has forbidden it.' Sophie turned to Philip. 'He is adamantly against the idea of celebrating Guy Fawkes' night. He thinks it's too dangerous to build a fire in the garden.'

'Perhaps I can persuade him,' Philip said. 'I promise I'll keep an eye on the children and make sure they're safe.'

'You can try,' Sophie said.

'Is Thomas at home now?'

'He's gone sick visiting but he'll be back for luncheon. Why don't you stay and talk to him?'

Sophie wasn't sure if she was doing the right thing in encouraging Philip, but she did not want the children to be disappointed. They had so looked forward to the excitement of a bonfire and staying up later than usual.

'Thank you, Sophie. I will stay. Perhaps the children and I can start building the fire now before he comes home. If I present him with a *fait accompli*, I am sure he won't refuse.'

Sophie smiled, amused by her brother's confidence in his powers of persuasion.

'We'll see,' she said, turning to the children. 'Well, run along then. Lessons are over for today.'

They did not need telling twice and in a flurry of donning coats, hats and scarves they flew out of the back door and were soon racing around the garden gathering up handfuls of twigs and small branches that had blown down in the recent storm.

Philip went down to the stable and spoke to Bill, who had been sawing up some of the larger branches. They began to stack the wood up in the centre of the lawn.

When Sophie looked out and saw what they were doing, she opened the window and called to them.

'Not there, Philip. Thomas will be furious if we spoil the lawn.'

'Where then?'

'Over to the side, but not too near the house.'

'I reckon about here will do, Ma'am,' Bill said, dragging a large branch over to where the wide herbaceous border had been dug out ready for the winter planting,

'Very well,' Sophie agreed, closing the window.

As she helped Ruby prepare the midday meal, she found her heart beating a little faster as she anticipated Thomas's return. She knew he would be very angry at the flouting of his command. As usual, she would bear the brunt of his displeasure but she was used to coping with that. It was the children's disappointment that she would find hard to take.

She tensed as she heard the sound of wheels on the driveway and the pony and trap appeared round the side of the house. She was tempted to go outside and try to intervene in the argument that she knew was about to ensue. But it would only make matters worse, especially if she took Philip's side.

Ruby announced that the dining room table was laid and the meal ready to dish up and Sophie went to call the children in. They were standing quietly beside the partially-built bonfire staring down the garden to where their father and uncle were in heated discussion.

'Amelia, go and tell your father that his luncheon is ready,' Sophie called. 'And you two, come inside and wash your hands.'

Edward was smiling as he came towards her.

'Mama, I think Uncle Philip has persuaded Father to change his mind about the bonfire. But he says we cannot have fireworks — they are much too dangerous.'

The smile left his face for a moment.

'I was so looking forward to them. But at least we can have a fire, and Uncle Philip says we can roast chestnuts in the embers.'

'That will be fun, dear.' Sophie was relieved that Thomas had given in. However, she couldn't help feeling that he might be right about the danger. Still, if they were careful ...

Besides, there would be plenty of adults around to supervise the children.

*   *   *

Bill the gardener had returned after his tea to help Philip with the bonfire and the two men were outside now making sure the huge pile of wood was secure before lighting it. As well as the branches from the pruned trees, they had added some pieces of broken furniture and old wooden boxes that had been stored in the shed beside the stable.

Indoors, Margaret and Sophie were getting the children into their outdoor clothes and ensuring that they were well wrapped up against the chill of the autumn evening.

'Stand still, Miss Amelia,' Margaret said. 'I'm trying to button your coat.'

'I can do it myself,' Amelia said.

'Very well,' Margaret sighed. Sophie looked at her in concern. She was usually so patient with the children.

At last they were ready and the children clattered downstairs and were out through the French windows before Sophie or Margaret could remonstrate with them.

Thomas was already outside on the terrace, watching the men build the fire.

'Don't go too close,' he called, as the children ran across the lawn. He turned to Sophie, frowning.

'They'll be all right,' she replied. 'Philip and Bill won't let them get too near.'

'Make sure they don't. I'm trusting you to keep an eye on your brother. He's little more than a child himself,' Thomas said. 'Well, I must finish my sermon.'

He went indoors abruptly, leaving Sophie seething. Why couldn't he enjoy spending some time with his children? If it wasn't for her brother's visits, they would never have any fun and they would grow up all too soon. But there was no use saying anything to her husband. He would not understand. She stifled her annoyance and turned to Margaret.

'Keep hold of Rosalind's hand, won't you?'

'Yes, Ma'am.' The nurse's reply came automatically and Sophie looked at her closely. Her eyes were sparkling with barely contained excitement and her cheeks were flushed. Was it just the prospect of spending a whole evening close to Philip that was affecting her?

Sophie bit her lip. She really ought to say something to the girl. She had tried remonstrating with her brother but it didn't seem to have had any effect. She stood watching for a few minutes as Philip and Margaret took the children's hands and started to dance around the bonfire, chanting, 'Remember, remember, the fifth of November ... '

It was good to see them enjoying themselves. She smiled and went indoors to check on Ruby and her preparations for supper. The girl had some large potatoes ready for roasting in the embers when the fire started to die down, and she had laid out cold meat and cooked sausages to go with them. If it was not too cold they would eat at the table on the terrace, a rare treat for the children, who would normally be in bed by the time the grown-ups had their supper.

'Bill's gathered some sweet chestnuts from the tree in the lane,' Ruby said. 'He'll roast those in the fire too.'

'I'm worried the children might burn their fingers,' Sophie confessed.

'Oh, no, Ma'am. Margaret will take care of them. You mustn't worry.'

Ruby spoke with the familiarity of long service with the family and Sophie forgave her for her outspokenness. Still, she couldn't help worrying. Although she had been pleased that Thomas had finally allowed the bonfire, there was a niggling feeling of apprehension at the back of her mind and it just would not go away.

Ruby brought the food out and Sophie called to Philip.

'Is it time to put the potatoes in the fire?'

He ran across the lawn, followed by the children.

'Yes, please, Mama,' they clamoured.

'Let me, let me,' Edward squealed.

'No, let your uncle do it. I promised your father you would not be allowed too near the fire.'

Edward scowled but obeyed, leaving Margaret and Philip to push the potatoes into the glowing embers. While they waited for the food to cook, Ruby poured hot milk from the jug and the children crept closer to the fire, cradling their hands round the mugs to ward off the chill.

Sophie watched them, content that the children were enjoying themselves without getting over-excited. And the grown-ups were behaving too, she noted. From time to time she stole a glance at her brother but, although he exchanged a few words with Margaret, she could detect nothing amiss in their manner towards each other.

Perhaps Philip had taken notice of her stern words and had decided that he must do his duty and honour his commitment to Alice. She could only hope. But still that feeling of impending disaster niggled at her.

18

As usual Clive was busy outside so Jo didn't have a chance to tell him about the proposed bonfire party. He was bound to pop in at coffee time and she'd talk to him then. Meantime there was plenty of work to do.

She picked up a creased and faded letter, struggling to make out the words.

'My dear Robert,' she read. She paused. Who the heck was Robert? She scrolled through the family tree on the computer until she reached the 1800s. There it was — Sophie's brother. She'd forgotten about him. But hadn't there been another brother too?

She read on.

'I was so pleased to hear from you, dear brother. At least you have not shunned me. I feared that my family had cut me off altogether when I decided to follow Philip out here. I know our parents have

never forgiven him for what happened and I was so sure that they blamed me for encouraging him that I felt I had no option but to go away too. I deeply regret leaving my husband but I could no longer bear his condemnation. I wish we could have comforted each other in our grief but he pushed me away. I do not blame him for this.'

Jo held the paper up to the light to try and make out the next words. But they were too blurred. Had the words been blotted out by Sophie's tears or was it just her imagination? she wondered. So many of the papers she'd been trying to catalogue were almost ruined by the damp in the attic where they had been stored. The next section was easier to read.

'I am so happy to hear that your health has improved and that you are now able to take care of the estate. And such happy news that you and Jane are soon to be parents — probably already are by the time you get this.

Philip is gradually recovering his health and spirits after the dreadful events of five years ago and now works hard on his land. He thinks there might be oil deposits and he has hired someone to drill down. He has started courting a local girl, the daughter of a neighbouring farmer, and I think that, although he will never forget Margaret, he may eventually find a little happiness.

Please continue to send me news of Grayling Manor. I miss you all so much and pray that we may all be together again one day.

Your loving sister, Sophie Blandford.'

Jo put the letter down and wiped her eyes with a tissue. What a sad story, she thought. A family torn apart by tragedy. She picked up the letter again and looked at the date — 1895. And it referred to something happening five years ago, something that the family blamed Philip and Sophie for. 1890 was the date on the children's graves; the same year Thomas Blandford had given up the living of St Mark's.

The children's deaths must be the dreadful event that Sophie was referring to. It didn't sound as though it was cholera, or one of the diseases so prevalent at the time. Why would Sophie's husband have condemned her for something beyond her control? Something else must have caused their deaths, and driven Sophie to leave her husband and flee abroad. Could it have been the fire, the one that destroyed St Mark's Rectory? Jo wondered, shuddering at the thought of those poor little ones, possibly trapped in that rambling old house.

And now she wondered, could those long ago events be the reason behind the strange happenings at the New Rectory? Although her common sense told her that such things were impossible, it was hard to ignore. Perhaps that would explain Lucy's morbid interest in the graveyard and her nocturnal wanderings. And there were those sounds Jo herself had heard — the voices of children singing in the garden, the sound of crying. When she had discovered that there were no children living in the houses down the lane, she had tried hard to convince herself that it had only been the sighing of the wind in the trees, or the creaks and groans to be found in so many old houses.

She laid the letter down on her desk and began to scrabble through the last lot of papers that Clive had brought down from the attic. She must find out the rest of the story.

The few remaining letters Jo managed to decipher didn't really tell her much. It seemed that Sophie had continued to write to her brother for some years but the tone of them became more despairing as time went on. She pleaded with Robert to persuade their parents to forgive Philip and allow him to return home. But it seemed it did no good. The time between letters grew longer and after a few years, ceased altogether.

'Did you know anything about this?' Jo asked, when Clive came in some time later.

'Not really. My mother hinted at something but I don't think she knew what had really happened. It was all such a long time ago and she wasn't interested in her family history at all.'

'If only we had the letters that Robert sent them. I don't suppose they passed anything onto you did they?'

'As I said, they weren't interested. And my great grandfather had made his own money. Our family didn't care about an inheritance from the old country.'

'It's hard to tell the whole story with only Sophie's letters to go on,' Jo said. 'It must have had something to do with the fire.'

'I think you're right,' Clive said. 'See, here she mentions Margaret again. She was the children's nursemaid.' He scrolled down and read out a portion of the letter.

'She always seemed devoted to the children but her infatuation with Philip overcame her sense of duty.'

'I think that's her grave in the church-yard — next to the children,' Jo said. 'What a tragic story.'

She sniffed and Clive touched her shoulder gently.

'It's sad, I know, but it's all in the past. Don't upset yourself.'

269

'I'm sorry. It's silly of me, isn't it? But it all seems so real, as if it happened only yesterday.'

'I feel the same, in a way. After all, it's my family we're talking about. Now I understand why people get so emotional on those television programmes where they're researching their ancestors.'

Jo was a little comforted by Clive's words. At least he understood. Some might have dismissed her reaction as being foolish.

'I expect it's because of the Grayling family's connection with the Rectory. It's brought your family history so much closer. It's not like researching an academic subject,' she said.

She attempted a smile and changed the subject.

'Talking of my house, I'm planning a house-warming now all the work's done. Lucy will be home and we've decided to have a bonfire party for Guy Fawkes' night. Would you like to come?'

She held her breath as she waited for his answer. Would he accept the transition from working relationship to a more personal one? She really hoped so.

He grinned. 'I'd love it. But you'll have to explain this Guy Fawkes thing. We don't celebrate that in Canada. Is it like Halloween?'

She told him the story of the gunpowder plot and how it had been celebrated ever since with bonfires and fireworks and he grinned. 'That's some history you have over here,' he said.

'Well, to be honest I don't think it's the history so much as the excuse for a party. Personally, I'm not keen on fireworks but my brother-in-law has promised he'll be very careful.'

'I suppose they can be dangerous,' Clive said. 'Especially with little kids around.'

'So, will you come?' Jo asked.

'Wouldn't miss it.'

Jo took a deep breath. 'Perhaps you could come early, before the family arrives? I thought you might like to have a look at the church where your ancestors worshipped. It all ties in with this story we've been researching.'

'That would be great. I must admit, I've got quite involved with this drama. When I started looking into the history of the Manor I thought it would all be to do with the running of the estate and the development of the building over the years.'

'The human story is much more fascinating, isn't it?' Jo said. As she spoke she felt a chill down her spine. Was she getting too involved with the Grayling story? Not to mention the strange feelings she'd experienced in and around the New Rectory.

The feeling went away almost immediately as Clive smiled and said, 'It will be nice to see you outside the work environment, get to know you better. You always seem so involved with the project. That's all we talk about.'

'I'd like that too,' Jo said quietly. She straightened her shoulders. 'Well, I'd better get on with this. A lot to get through, still.'

'There you go again, all business. Take a break, Jo.' He held out a hand and pulled her up out of the chair. 'Come on, get your coat. It's a bit chilly out but the sun's shining. I want to show you how the work on the stable is getting on.'

Now *he's* being businesslike, Jo thought, as he helped her on with her coat. He just wants an audience to show off what he's achieved so far. But as he held the door open for her, he took her hand and did not let go as they strolled round the stable yard.

'I want to show you my plans for outbuildings,' he said. 'They're making the old stables weatherproof so that we can store all the reclaimable furniture and fittings here until the house is finished.'

The foreman came towards them and Clive asked how the roof was coming along.

'OK, boss. Just need to fix these doors now.'

'Good. Looks like we're just in time before the winter sets in,' Clive said.

As they strolled round the cobbled stable yard, he became more excited as he told Jo about his plans.

'A tea room in the stables, perhaps a shop too.'

'It sounds wonderful,' Jo said, smiling at his enthusiasm.

'Let's go inside and I'll show you the plans.'

They walked back towards the house and he continued to talk excitedly about his plans.

'Once the buildings are all sorted I'll start on the grounds. I want to restore the walled garden.'

Jo listened in silence, her heart sinking as she realised that all too soon her job would come to an end.

'I suppose once the cataloguing is finished, you won't need me any more.'

He still had hold of her hand and he pulled her round to face him.

'Of course I will,' he said. 'There will still be loads of stuff to do. The guide-book, brochures.'

For a moment Jo had dared to hope that he meant he needed her for something other than work. But he dropped her hand and held the door open for her.

Disappointed, she went to move past him, but he placed a hand on her shoulder and gently pulled her towards him. As he bent his head to kiss her, thoughts of her daughter's disapproval intruded, but she couldn't deny that this was what she wanted. She leaned in to him and gave herself up to the delightful sensation of his arms around her and his lips exploring hers. It had been far too long.

* * *

For the next couple of days she hardly saw Clive and wondered if he was avoiding her, regretting that impulsive kiss. Would he turn up for the bonfire party? she wondered.

As she prepared the food she kept glancing at the clock, a frisson of excitement churning her stomach at the thought of entertaining him in her own home. She had been dying to invite him for ages but had been wary of giving her feelings away. A party with other people present would be a good introduction to her home and family, she'd thought. And perhaps she would be able to gauge if that kiss had meant anything. She dearly hoped so. She was ready to move on. She just hoped that Lucy would accept that her mother deserved a little happiness after the lonely years without Tom.

She was mixing the salad dressing, lost in thought, when a knock came at the door. Was that Clive already? Heart thumping, she went to let him in.

'I'm not too early, am I?' he asked.

'Not at all,' she said, stammering a little. 'Come in. I'll just finish this and then we can go over to the church.'

Although Ben had tried to fill in the gap in the hedge, every time the children came over to play, they opened it up again and Jo had given up trying to stop them going into the churchyard. Now she pushed her way through, beckoning to Clive to follow.

As they walked round to the porch, she pointed out the row of little graves. He bent to examine the names and turned to face her, his face solemn. 'So, my great-grandfather would have been their uncle?' he said.

'I'm sure of it, going by the letters Sophie sent.'

'And she was their mother. What a tragedy — to lose all one's children like that.'

Jo unlocked the church door and stepped into the porch. The familiar smell of damp and mould assailed her and she shivered, wishing she was back in the warmth of her kitchen. But Clive had walked down the side aisle to examine the board with its list of rectors going back to the 1300s.

'So much history here,' he said. 'We've nothing like this in Canada.' He pointed to the name near the bottom of the list. 'Thomas Blandford — Sophie's husband. He must have left his position as rector after the fire.'

'I haven't found anything about him in the records so far,' Jo said. 'I suppose his wife leaving him was a scandal in those days.'

Clive shook his head.

'Let's get out of here. This place is getting to me. I think we've spent too much time dwelling on this tragedy.'

He grabbed her hand and ran her up the aisle and out through the porch. Outside in the weak autumn sunshine he pulled her towards him and leaned in for a kiss.

Thoughts of ancestors and history fled as Jo gave herself up to his embrace. But just as she was wishing they could stay like that forever, Clive drew away. He put his head on one side, listening.

'Was that a car I heard? I do believe your guests are arriving.' He laughed. 'Come on, it's party time. Let's have some fun.'

And it *was* fun. Clive and Mike hit it off straight away and set about organising the fireworks between them. Jo was happy to see that Ben and Lucy spent most of the time with their arms around each other. They had obviously been missing each other while Lucy was away. Jack shot jealous glances at them from time to time but appeared to be happy helping to entertain the children, lighting their sparklers for them and making sure they did not get too near the fire.

When Liz and Jo went indoors to fetch the food, Liz said, 'You're looking very smug. Is it Clive?'

Jo blushed and nodded.

'Really? Oh, Jo! I'm so pleased for you. He seems so nice and you have such a lot in common.'

'But how will Lucy feel about me in a new relationship?'

'You worry too much. She'll be fine. And if she's not, she'll get over it.' Liz gave her sister a hug. 'Lucy's a big girl and she's making her own life. You deserve to be able to get on with yours too.'

'I suppose you're right,' Jo said.

'I know I am. Now, come on, let's get this food out. They'll be starving.'

★ ★ ★

Later, as the fire died down, they ate the hot baked potatoes and sausages. Jack sat on the swing and played his guitar.

Jo, seated on a garden bench with Clive's arm around her shoulders, sighed contentedly until she saw Lucy watching them. She made to move away, but Lucy shook her head, grinning, and gave her mother a thumbs-up sign.

It was getting late and Jo knew the children were getting tired, but she didn't want the evening to end. At that moment, though, Liz clapped her hands.

'Come on kids, time you were in bed,' she called.

There were collective groans and Amy said, 'One more game, please, Mummy.'

Liz gave a resigned sigh.

'Never mind,' said Mike, 'they'll be tired out tomorrow and we can have a lie-in.'

Amy grabbed her brother and sister's hands and they began to circle the bonfire, chanting, 'Ladybird, ladybird, fly away home, the house is on fire and your children all gone.'

Jo smiled as she watched the children and was about to turn and say something to Clive when she realised what they were singing. The words sent a chill down her spine.

She was about to call out to them to stop when everything began to blur before her eyes as if a sudden mist had got up. She could still see the children dancing but they had been joined by a young woman in a long dress, her hair in braids round her head. And there was a young man with them — not Jack or Ben but a tall, dark-haired man in riding breeches and jacket, with a white stock at his throat. Who were they?

As she slid to the ground in a faint, she became aware of Clive bending over her, his face creased in concern. He chafed her hands between his, urging her to wake up.

'Jo, what's wrong? Speak to me, please.'

She struggled to sit up.

'I'm all right,' she said, glancing round. 'Where are they?'

'Who?'

'Those people.'

'There's no one here apart from us, Jo,' Liz said.

'I saw them,' Jo protested.

Lucy laughed. 'Perhaps it was the ghosts.'

Liz rounded on her. 'This is no joke, Lucy. Your mum's obviously not well. Let's help her into the house.'

'Sorry.' Lucy took Jo's arm and helped her up.

As she supported her mother inside, with Clive hovering anxiously behind, Jo whispered to her daughter, 'I'm the one who should be sorry. I think you're right. They weren't real people I saw.'

Jo had tried so hard to convince herself that all the odd events surrounding the Rectory must have a rational explanation, but she was sure that tonight she really had seen a vision from the past. Who would ever believe her, though?

Clive urged her to sit down. 'I'll get you a drink,' he said.

'I'm all right now. The others are leaving. I must go and see them off.'

But she still felt shaky and she was glad of Clive's arm around her.

The children were running around outside, seemingly oblivious to their aunt's distress, while Mike, Ben and Jack were damping down the bonfire. Liz called the children over and insisted they must go home.

'I'm off now too,' Jack said.

'Mum's seen a ghost,' Lucy announced. 'Told you the house was haunted.'

'So there's something in those old stories my gran told us,' Jack said, laughing. He slung his guitar over his shoulder, and giving a last kick at the smouldering embers of the fire, disappeared round the side of the house.

'What an ending to the party,' Jo said, trying to laugh.

But the evening wasn't quite over.

19

1890

The children were in bed, tired out after the excitement of the bonfire party. Although Thomas had vetoed having fireworks, Philip had produced some small sticks, which he lit at the ends. The children shrieked with delight as they waved them around, producing a flurry of sparkles. Sophie had gasped at the sight but Philip had assured her they were quite safe.

As she prepared for bed she heaved a sigh of relief that all had gone well. The children had been well-behaved, Thomas had stayed closeted in his study, and Philip had only spoken to Margaret when necessary. In fact, it had seemed to her that he had almost been ignoring her, although from time to time she had caught the nursemaid stealing glances at him. Was her brother really resolved to be sensible at last? Sophie wondered.

Thomas was already asleep and, as Sophie was about to join him in bed, she thought she heard a noise from outside. She paused. There it was again.

It had been a calm, still night so far, but as she listened, she realised the wind had got up and was gusting noisily. That's what it must have been, she told herself, going to the window and pulling the curtain aside. She looked down at the front garden and the lane beyond, just visible in the faint moonlight. But she could see nothing there.

She shrugged and let the curtain fall just as the noise came again, this time from the back of the house. That wasn't the wind, she thought. It sounded like the stable door banging. Had Bill forgotten to shut it properly when Philip left on his horse? Or was someone out there? Perhaps she should rouse Thomas.

She shook his shoulder but he grunted and turned over. I'll just have to look myself, she thought, knowing she would never get to sleep if she ignored it. Pulling her wrapper around her and tying the belt, she went out on to the landing and quietly opened the door to the nursery, smiling at the sight of the children fast asleep. Nothing would disturb them to-night, exhausted as they were after their unaccustomed late bedtime.

She crept downstairs and unbolted the back door, careful to make no noise. If she saw any cause for alarm she would run back upstairs and force Thomas awake. She stood by the open door for several minutes but heard nothing and she was about to return to her room when a fleeting movement out of the corner of her eye made her pause. Someone was creeping alongside the hedge which bordered the churchyard, making for the stable at the end of the garden.

Surely it wasn't Philip. He had gone home hours ago. The figure straightened, and her relief that her brother had not returned for an assignation with the nurse-maid was tempered by the realisation that this could be a burglar. She stifled a gasp and almost called out. But she thrust her fist in her mouth as the clouds parted and the moon shone full on his face. It was Joe, the blacksmith's apprentice, who had been pursuing Margaret for weeks. What was he doing here?

Perhaps he had arranged to meet the nursemaid after the household was all asleep. Although Sophie could not condone such behaviour, she couldn't help being a little relieved that perhaps the girl was beginning to realise how impossible a relationship with Philip would be. If she had agreed to meet Joe, perhaps that was why she and Philip had seemed to be avoiding each other earlier in the evening.

I must put a stop to this though, she decided. If Joe wants to court Margaret he must do it openly and in a proper manner, not clandestinely after midnight. She could scarcely believe that the nursemaid would agree to meet him outside the house. She only hoped she could intervene and send Joe home before Thomas woke and found out what was going on.

She waited a few moments until the man was further down the garden and then followed him down the path. He pushed open the stable door and she crept closer, just in time to hear angry voices. To her horror she realised Philip was there too. The sound of blows and a high-pitched scream rent the air.

Sophie entered the building to see Margaret cowering against the wall, her hands over her face, sobbing.

'Stop them, please,' she wailed.

Sophie put her arms around the girl and tried to lead her outside, but Margaret resisted. The men were still fighting, rolling around on the straw-covered floor. Joe pulled Philip to his feet and hit out at him, causing him to stagger backwards, his arms flailing.

'Stop it, both of you,' Sophie cried but they ignored her, continuing to aim blows at each other. She put her arms around Margaret and said, 'Leave them to it. I'll go and fetch the master. He'll put a stop to this nonsense.'

'No, please, Ma'am. It's not Philip's

fault. I told Joe I didn't want to see him. It's Philip I love.' She reached out towards the men and tried to grab Joe's arm. 'Let him go, please. I told you I didn't want any trouble.'

Joe shook her off and pushed Philip outside where they continued the fight.

Sophie followed them and glanced up at the house, hoping to see a light. Surely Thomas must have heard something and would come down and intervene. But the Rectory was still in darkness.

By now Philip had got the best of it and stood over Joe, snarling.

'You'd better be off before the Rector catches you here. I wouldn't give any chances of you keeping your job once he tells your master what you've been up to.'

Joe wiped a hand across his bloody mouth and sneered.

'O' course, everyone will take the word of a Grayling, won't they.' He stumbled across the lawn, turning to fling a last threat. 'You haven't heard the last of this, mark my words.' He kicked out viciously at the remains of the bonfire, sending up a shower of smouldering flakes of debris. Then he disappeared through a gap in the hedge.

Sophie, her arms still around the nursemaid, threw an angry look at her brother.

'What do you think you were up to, sneaking back here so late?'

'We were leaving.' He turned to Margaret. 'Fetch your bag, my love.'

'Leaving? Where do you think you are going?' Sophie shouldn't have been shocked, should have seen what was coming, but she could scarcely believe that her children's beloved nursemaid would elope and leave her charges. As for her brother, she had known how irresponsible he could be but she had always believed that a sense of duty would eventually overcome his infatuation.

Margaret had gone back into the stable and returned carrying a carpet bag.

'I'm ready,' she said, handing him the bag.

'No, you mustn't,' Sophie said. 'It's wrong.'

'You can't stop us. Our minds are

made up,' Philip said, taking Margaret's hand.

Anger fought with sorrow in Sophie's mind at the thought of two young lives ruined by scandal. But she couldn't help a sneaking feeling of sympathy at the same time, remembering how different her own life could have been if she had followed her heart.

Her shoulders slumped and she spoke quietly.

'I can't condone what you are doing, but I can wish you all the best and hope that you find happiness.' She reached up and kissed Philip's cheek and he embraced her, hugging her tight.

'I'll be in touch, let you know where we are,' he said. 'I don't suppose the rest of the family will want anything to do with me from now on.'

Margaret looked up at Sophie with a wistful smile.

'I'm so sorry, Ma'am. I did not mean to cause all this trouble. You won't let the children think badly of me, will you?'

Sophie could not reply, just waved them away. She was about to turn back towards the house, when Margaret gasped and cried out.

'What is it?'

'The fire,' Philip shouted.

A gust of wind had caught the embers stirred up by Joe's boot and the bonfire had flared up. Flakes of burning debris were flying in the air. Margaret and Sophie stood helplessly by as the wind gusted more violently, and they realised the embers had reached the house.

'Philip, fetch water before it's too late,' Sophie said, running towards the pump in the stable yard. Already the burning debris was setting fire to the timbers in the old house. Flames reared up around the windows as they frantically pumped water into buckets and tried to stem the blaze.

'The children,' Sophie gasped. 'We must get them out.' She ran towards the kitchen door. 'Margaret — help me.' But the girl had disappeared.

Philip was still trying to pour water

on the flames but they could see it was already too late.

'Leave it,' Sophie cried. 'Get the children. I'll wake Thomas.'

But as they tried to enter the house they were beaten back by smoke and flames.

'Stay here,' Philip commanded. 'I'll get them. Margaret must be inside too.'

He leapt through the doorway and disappeared.

20

Liz and her family had gone home and Jo was sitting in front of the wood burner, wrapped in a blanket and sipping from a glass of water. She had assured everyone that she was quite recovered from her fainting spell, laughingly dismissing the talk of ghostly apparitions.

'It was the heat from the bonfire,' she said. 'And I've been spending so much time lately thinking about the Blandfords, that lived here before. It was preying on my mind.'

Clive put a hand on her shoulder.

'I didn't see anything, but I believe you were right the first time,' he said. 'I lived among the native Americans in northern Canada and learned about their spiritual beliefs. There are truly some things which defy rational explanation.'

'Thank you,' Jo whispered. 'I was beginning to think I was ... ' Her voice trailed away and she bit her lip.

'You've had a shock. Would you like me to stay?' Clive asked.

There was nothing Jo wanted more, but she shook her head. She would have agreed if Lucy hadn't been there but she couldn't cope with her daughter's possible reaction to a man staying the night.

'I'll be OK,' she said.

'I'd better be off then — if you're sure.' He went to the door, pausing to look back at her, then turned and left abruptly.

She sighed and wished she had risked Lucy's disapproval. She would have to try and explain when she saw Clive at work on Monday.

Lucy was about to say something but Jo couldn't cope with any more. She stood up and discarded the blanket.

'I'm off to bed,' she said.

'I'll just see Ben out, then,' Lucy said.

At that moment the door burst open and Clive erupted into the room.

'Quick — there's a fire.' He hustled them out through the kitchen before they had time to take in his words.

Outside, Jo looked around in confusion. Surely Mike and Jack had damped down the bonfire before leaving? She was sure it had been completely extinguished before she went inside. It must have been as Jack kicked the fire, disturbing the embers — that was the only explanation she could think of. She realised she had been aware of the smell of smoke for some time but she had put it down to the lingering smell from the fireworks.

'Where is it?' she asked looking down the garden to where they'd been dancing such a short time before.

'There,' Clive shouted, pointing over her shoulder towards the roof of the house.

Now she could see flames leaping and hear the crackle of and roar of the fire.

'I've called 999 for the fire brigade,' Lucy said and Jo blessed her for being so welded to her mobile. She had not thought to grab hers as Clive had hustled them outside. 'It must have been Jack kicking the embers as he left.'

She gazed up at the house, mesmerised by the smoke and flames, swaying on her feet as her eyes blurred once more.

She could hear Clive's anxious voice but above it and the noise of the fire she could hear crying.

'The children,' she gasped, shaking off Clive's restraining hand and running towards the house.

She raced up the stairs, which were already wreathed in smoke, coughing. At the top, a wall of flame greeted her and she reeled back. Clive was right behind her and he pulled her away, almost carrying her down the stairs.

Lucy and Ben rushed towards them as he laid her down on the grass outside.

'Mum, what were you thinking of?' Lucy gasped, tears running down her face. Ben put his arms round her and comforted her as Clive knelt beside Jo, begging her to open her eyes.

'Jo, are you all right? Speak to me,' he implored.

As she became aware of him and struggled to sit up, a puzzled frown crossed her face. A bearded stranger dressed in a long coat stared down at her.

'Who are you?' she whispered.

'It's me, Clive.'

The stranger's face receded and her vision cleared. With a shaky laugh, she shook her head and she reached out to touch his face.

'You rescued me,' she murmured.

'What on earth made you run back inside?' he asked.

'The children.' Her eyes widened and she looked round frantically.

'They went home ages ago. There're no children here,' Clive said.

'You mean the other children, don't you, Mum?' Lucy said. 'The ones over there.' She nodded her head towards the churchyard.

Jo didn't reply.

★   ★   ★

After the firemen had tackled the blaze, and got it under control, the Chief Fire Officer came over and asked if Jo needed to go to hospital.

'I'm fine, thanks to Clive,' she said, smiling at him and holding tightly to his hand.

'We've made it safe for now, but one of my men will stay and make sure it doesn't flare up again.'

'Is it safe to go back in?' Lucy asked.

'Not a chance right now,' he replied. 'Do you have somewhere to go?'

'Lucy can come home with me,' Ben said, putting a protective arm around her.

'Mum?' Lucy said.

'Go on, love. I'll be OK. I'll phone Liz.'

'No need. You can come back to the Manor,' Clive said. 'There's plenty of room.'

'Are you sure?' Jo looked up at him, hoping there was more to his invitation than just being helpful. She smiled when she could see in his eyes that her hopes were not in vain.

He helped her to her feet and put his arm around her.

'We'd better get going,' he said.

Lucy came over and gave her mother a hug.

'I knew it. Go for it, Mum,' she whispered.

'Are you sure you don't mind?'

Lucy kissed her cheek. 'I just want you to be happy.'

Jo looked back at the ruins of the house she had so lovingly restored but she felt no regret. It was as if the story of the New Rectory had come full circle.

Her daughter smiled dreamily.

'I think it was meant to be. It feels like the children are at peace now.' Lucy looked round at the gutted house and the gardens; she frowned as her gaze alighted on the tree at the bottom of the garden.

'That's odd. Where's the swing gone?'

21

1890

Thomas solemnly intoned the final words of the burial service and closed his prayer book. With a sob, Sophie turned to him, reaching out an imploring hand, but he turned away, his face an impassive mask, and re-entered the church. She stood looking down at the tiny graves, tears pouring down her cheeks — tears which she made no attempt to wipe away.

Robert and Jane, standing on either side of her, tried to lead her away.

'Come along, Sophie,' Jane urged. 'Let's take you home.'

'Home? I have no home now,' she said, giving a last glance back at the final resting place of her children, and shuddering at the sight of yet another freshly dug grave alongside them. Finally, she allowed herself to be helped along the narrow path to where the carriage waited. Her parents were already seated inside but neither of them spoke.

They blame me, she thought. So does Thomas. If I hadn't kept Margaret on, if I'd dismissed her as soon as I realised what was going on, this would never have happened. She held a handkerchief to her face, trying to blot out the smell of the still-smouldering remains of the house on the other side of the churchyard.

It had all happened so quickly. After Philip had dashed into the house, she realised that Margaret had also gone in. She had tried to follow them, screaming out the names of her children. But she had been beaten back by the flames and rolling clouds of black smoke.

She gasped with relief when a figure appeared in the doorway. It was Thomas. She should have been relieved but she had not spared him a thought once she realised the children were in danger. He had Amelia in his arms and she ran up to him.

'Is she all right?' she cried.

He shook his head and laid the small bundle down on the grass. He attempted to go back into the house but Philip staggered out, shaking his head. 'It's no use,' he sobbed.

He sank down onto the grass and covered his face with his hands, groaning with pain.

As the carriage bowled along the country lanes towards the Manor, Sophie replayed the scene in her head as she had so many times over the past few days. Was there anything more she could have done, she asked herself.

She dried her eyes and tried to make conversation.

'It was a lovely service. It must have been hard for Thomas,' she said.

'He does these things very well,' her mother replied. 'Still, it is his job after all.'

'Will he be coming back to the Manor?' her father asked.

'I don't know. He has scarcely spoken to me since it happened.' Sophie gave another little sob. 'He cannot forgive me.'

Jane attempted to comfort her. 'There is nothing to forgive. From what Philip tells me, you tried to rescue them — as did he. It was a tragic accident.'

Sophie's mother spoke up sharply.

'Do not mention that name in my hearing ever again, Jane. It was my son's ... ' She almost choked on the word. ' ... my son's unseemly behaviour that caused all this. The very idea — a Grayling eloping with a maid servant.'

James covered his wife's hand with his own.

'Do not distress yourself, my dear. He will be gone soon and the scandal will soon be forgotten.'

That's all they are worried about, Sophie thought, the scandal. Never mind their grandchildren. And what about me? I have lost my whole family, not just the children, but Thomas too, it seems — and Philip, my beloved little brother. When he sails for Canada, I will surely never see him again.

22

Back at the Manor, Clive settled Jo into an armchair in front of the log fire, tucked a rug around her knees and poured her a tot of brandy.

'This will help you feel better,' he said.

Jo would have preferred a cup of tea but she sipped the spirit, grateful for the warmth it imparted. She still couldn't stop shaking as she realised how narrowly a tragedy had been averted — a tragedy that would have mirrored the one so long ago.

Now the letters and photographs she had been studying made sense. The story she had pieced together told of a family torn apart by a young man's infatuation and their reaction to what they saw as his scandalous behaviour.

Despite her firm assertion that she did not believe in the supernatural, she could not deny the truth of the strange happenings since she had moved into the New Rectory. And she had to admit that it had probably been brought about by her close connection with the Manor and her delving into its archives.

Her thoughts were still chaotic as she sipped the brandy but it was having a calming effect and she looked up to see Clive watching her.

'Are you sure you're OK?' he asked.

She nodded. 'Thanks to you,' she whispered.

'Don't ever do anything like that again,' he said. 'When I saw you rushing into the house ... ' He knelt beside her and took her hand. 'I thought I'd lost you. I couldn't bear it if ... ' His voice broke.

She pulled her hand away and reached up to caress his cheek. 'You won't lose me,' she said. 'I'm here, aren't I?'

'And you'll stay?'

'I'll stay,' she said.

He removed the brandy glass from her hand and his arms encircled her. The kiss that followed was all she had dreamt of, and the events of the evening, as well as those of that long ago autumn night, faded from her mind.

We do hope that you have enjoyed reading this large print book.

Did you know that all of our titles are available for purchase?

We publish a wide range of high quality large print books including:
Romances, Mysteries, Classics
General Fiction
Non Fiction and Westerns

Special interest titles available in large print are:
The Little Oxford Dictionary
Music Book, Song Book
Hymn Book, Service Book

Also available from us courtesy of Oxford University Press:
Young Readers' Dictionary
(large print edition)
Young Readers' Thesaurus
(large print edition)

For further information or a free brochure, please contact us at:
Ulverscroft Large Print Books Ltd.,
The Green, Bradgate Road, Anstey,
Leicester, LE7 7FU, England.
Tel: (00 44) **0116 236 4325**
Fax: (00 44) **0116 234 0205**

SUMMER'S DREAM

Jean M. Long

Talented designer Juliet Croft is devastated when the company she works for closes. She takes a temporary job at the Linden Manor Hotel, but soon hears rumours that the business is in financial difficulties — and suspects that Sheldon's, a rival company, is involved. During her work, she renews her friendship with Scott, a former colleague. At the same time, she must cope with her growing feelings for Martin Glover, the hotel manager. Trouble is, he's already taken . . .

SEEING SHADOWS

Susan Udy

Lexie Brookes is busy running her hairdressing salon and wondering what to do about her cooling relationship with her partner, Danny. When the jewellery shop next door is broken into via her own premises, the owner — the wealthy and infuriatingly arrogant Bruno Cavendish — blames her for his losses. Then Danny disappears, and Lexie is suddenly targeted by a mysterious stalker. To add to the turmoil, Bruno appears to be attracted to her, and she finds herself equally drawn to him . . .

A DATE WITH ROMANCE

Toni Anders

Refusing to live in the shadow of her father, a famous TV chef, Lauren Tate runs her own cake shop with her best friend, Daisy. Having been unlucky in love, Lauren pours her energy into her business — until she meets her handsome new neighbour, Jake, who is keen to strike up a friendship with her. Will Lauren decide to take him up on the offer? Then Daisy has an accident, and announces she'll be following her partner to America once she has healed — leaving Lauren with some difficult choices . . .

ALL BECAUSE OF BAXTER

Sharon Booth

When Ellie's marriage unexpectedly ends, she and her young son Jacob seek refuge with Ellie's cousin Angie. But Angie soon tires of her house guests, including her own boisterous rescue dog, Baxter. When Baxter literally bumps into Dylan, Ellie dares to dream of a happy ending at last. But time is running out for them, and it seems Dylan has a secret that may jeopardise everything. Must Ellie give up on her dreams, or can Baxter save the day?

FESTIVAL FEVER

Margaret Mounsdon

Fleur Denman is given the chance of a lifetime to front the Ridgly Parva Arts and History Festival — but some locals have long memories, and aren't prepared to overlook the scandal that once blackened the Denman name. In the face of adversity, Fleur sets out to prove her worth. Then some festival money goes missing, and Ben Salt, the main sponsor, is among the first to point an accusing finger in her direction. To make matters worse, Fleur finds herself increasingly attracted to him . . .

HEART OF THE MOUNTAIN

Carol MacLean

Emotionally burned out from her job as a nurse, Beth leaves London for the Scottish Highlands and the peace of her aunt's cottage. Here she meets Alex, a man who is determined to live life to the full after the death of his fiancée in a climbing accident. Despite her wish for a quiet life, Beth is pulled into a friendship with Alex's sister, bubbly Sarah-Jayne, and finds herself increasingly drawn to Alex . . .